The Skull

T. D. Deinstadt

Copyright © 2023 T.D.Deinstadt

All rights reserved.

ISBN: 9798377296812

Dedicated to my mother Christine Deinstadt. For everything you have done in my life and everything you will do in my life. Thank you.

CONTENTS

	Acknowledgments	i
	Prologue	Pg 1
1	Appearance	Pg 4
2	Panic	Pg 63
3	What Now?	Pg 76
4	Hit the Fan	Pg 117
5	Home	Pg 142
6	Stalled	Pg 166
7	Lemons	Pg 178
8	Plotting	Pg 213
9	Finale	Pg 224
	Epilogue	Pg 236
	About the Author	Pg 241

ACKNOWLEDGMENTS

I would like to acknowledge my mother again for all the hard work she does to put up with me. Also, my siblings because they will complain if I don't acknowledge their presence. I have evidence of this.

PROLOGUE

I was three when I learned what the tattoos meant. All the adults had them. I remember the one that just appeared one day on my mother's stomach. She had two there already. One was a little kitten curled up sleeping in what looked like sunlight. The other was a Celtic knot of the oak. Supposedly it represents courage. The new one that appeared was a skull. No one understood the meaning. They just knew that mom was pregnant again. I didn't understand until dad sat us down and explained that we were going to have a little sister or brother.

When you get older you get a tattoo that appears on the back of your neck that's identical to the one on your mother. It usually shows up just before you hit puberty. That's when you start learning the meanings of different tattoos in school. I now understood that my sister was that little kitten tattoo. She grew up to be sleek and sophisticated, there were even times when she seemed to move like a cat. Still whenever there's a warm beam of sunshine she has a habit of flopping down and taking a long nap. I was the Celtic knot. Mother always said I looked Fae. I do have ears that appear to be more pointed than the norm. I'm also super tiny. I had barely hit 4 foot 5 when my body decided it was done growing. I normally shop in the kids sections or I have to get clothes specially made for me. It's a pain but one I've always lived with.

My brother was the skull. After mom lost him we understood the meaning. Skull = Death. There's no cheating death. Which is why when a skull showed up on the inside of my left forearm I began to panic.

1 APPEARANCE

2 Days before the skull appeared

Annie and Jim are going at it again. They just can't get past making a decision together. If one wants to serve coffee the other will demand they serve tea. It doesn't really matter. I'll make the call and the shop will serve both. That's my job. To make both the owners happy. I've known Annie and Jim since high school. We all worked at various coffee shops together. When it came time to leave college Annie and Jim took their trust funds and started their own shop. They hired me to do the hard stuff. Sourcing product, getting store fronts set up, hiring and training staff. Making them get along. I was ok with all that. They're my friends, they pay well and I have a great benefits package. Which makes sense since I'm the one who builds the packages.

The shop was a huge hit. After it took off Annie and Jim got married. Ever since then they've been determined to find someone for me. I take my seat at the table and hope that they will finish their argument without me needing to interfere.

"Really Jim! We're a coffee shop! No offense but getting a liquor license turns us into a bar!" as I watch Annie flip her bottle blonde hair over her shoulder I notice a new mark slowly materialize along her neck and up towards her ear.

"Honey just hear me out! If we got a license we could serve specialized coffee and tea based cocktails! No one's doing it yet - we'd corner the market!" Jim still hasn't noticed the change taking place in Annie yet, odd, he's usually the one who is first to see these kinds of things. Even before Annie herself notices.

The new mark on Annie curls behind her ear and begins to take shape as a flower vine. Suddenly little pink buds start appearing. Neither of them seem to have noticed my arrival. They're too involved in their argument. With a sigh I know I need to speak up.

"Hey guys, how about I do some research and see if the business would be able to support Jim's idea first. Then once we have the numbers we can look at the notion again with fresh eyes?" I really just wanted this meeting done. We were supposed to be looking at ways to keep the whole business fresh and relevant. If the argument went on much longer I'd be late meeting my sister for lunch. She's been teasing me for days now - apparently she has some big news but she wants to tell me in person. Annie and Jim are both staring at me now. Neither one looks pleased that I interrupted them, there must be something more going on here than just the usual tiff. I look away with the hope that they will stop staring at me like I was something they could tear apart. Slowly they go back to shouting at each other. Out of boredom I begin to trace the coffee vine tattoo on the back of my left hand. It appeared the day that Annie and Jim came up with the idea to open a coffee shop. I didn't know until class on Monday that they had identical tattoos to mine on their hands.

"You know what? *Fine!* I'll go only as far as letting Dawn do the research. It'll be a waste of time for her but at least numbers might convince you that this is a bad idea!"

"And if the numbers are good then I'm going forward no matter how much you don't like it!" Jim's roar echoed for a moment before he slammed the door as he stormed out of the room.

"*Ugh*! He's impossible! Never go into business with your spouse! I swear he just does stuff like this to make me angry!" Annie ranted on this way for a good half hour before I could get a word in edgewise. At least she wasn't bright red with anger anymore.

"If you don't mind my asking, where did he get this idea anyways?" Maybe if I knew I'd have better luck navigating this into something better for all of us and the company.

"A tattoo. Last night it appeared. You know where our vines are? A bottle of Kahlua just materialized in amongst the vines. They rearranged to accommodate the bottle. Jim thinks that this is what it means," Annie finally stopped pacing around and sat down. Her hand was subconsciously rubbing where the new mark on Jim was.

"What do you think it means?"

"That he drinks too much. I've tried talking him into getting help but he doesn't think he has an issue."

"Ok. What do you think your new tattoo means?"

"Huh?" sheer confusion on her face. It seems Annie didn't even feel the tattoo appear this time. I fished my compact out of my bag and handed it to her, showing her on my own neck where her tattoo has appeared. "I don't know. I can't tell what kind of flower that is, unlike Jim I'm not going to jump to any conclusions though."

She handed me back my compact but now she also won't make eye contact with me. As I put it away I do my best to unobtrusively observe her. Her roots are beginning to show her natural mouse brown hair colour. Her make up is always spot on, even when she cries, she tends to look perfect. She's matched her blouse to her brown eyes. There's something off though - she's blushing. I know it can't be because she said something insulting about Jim, or that I was in the middle of their arguments. I've been doing that for years. There's something else going on. It's Annie though. If she doesn't want to volunteer the information yet I won't pry. She'll tell me in her own time.

"Look, since Jim is out of here already why don't I leave a copy of the refresh ideas with you and you can go over them. Email me when you're done and then leave them on Jim's desk for him. Then I'll do the research for his idea and that will give us something to compare with," a quick glance at the clock and I know I'm already late for lunch.

"Sure, sounds good," Annie seemed very subdued at this point but I don't have time to reassure her that everything will be fine. I handed over the folders I had put together and got up to leave.

"I'm having lunch with my sister so I may be a little late getting back in the office."

"Don't worry about it, you put in more time here than anyone else. Even Jim and I."

"Thanks Annie. I'll see you later."

It's raining outside. Thankfully I do have a decent jacket - even if I didn't bring an umbrella. The restaurant is just around the corner from the office, maybe a block or two away at most. Still, I'm nearly soaked by the time I arrive. My sister has already ordered for us both. Not my preferred meal (I like chicken tenders and grilled cheese anywhere) but at least the soup is warm and filling.

"Who knew spring could be this chilly!" Lynn said as I took my first few sips of the soup. Even in her most casual of clothes she looks sleek. Apparently a rumpled turtleneck shirt and ripped up jeans can look like a couture outfit if you're tall and thin.

"Well, it is still pretty early. Give it a couple weeks. So, what's your big news?"

"I'm pregnant."

"No! Really? What kind of tattoo?" I love the idea of being an auntie. I never really had anyone romantically interested in me so I never saw myself having kids. My sister has been married a little over three years. Her husband has a job in some tech company. There was plenty of money so my sister didn't need to work.

"It's a little whale," Lynn was absolutely glowing with joy.

"So, a big baby," I couldn't help but tease her a little. Mom always said that her little kitten had been huge.

We chatted for a while longer and finished up our lunches. I was happy. The day had started out so poorly and now nothing could rock me out of my good mood, not even the rain. Except…. seeing Annie kissing someone that most certainly wasn't Jim a block and a half away from the office.

At first I wasn't certain it was her. Then I noticed the vines. Both on her neck and hand. There's no mistaking them. After doing my best to get a good look at him without being conspicuous, I turned and jogged the rest of the way back to the office. If I was lucky, I would be able to get the few things I needed so I could work the rest of the day from home without running in to either Annie or Jim.

Luck is no friend of mine. If it had been maybe I'd have grown a four leaf clover. No. Barely in the doorway when I run smack in to Jim. And guess who he was looking for.

"Dawn, have you seen Annie? I can't find her anywhere," his grey eyes locked on to me.

"I think I saw her a few blocks from here. I had lunch with my sister and was on my way back. She probably just ran out to grab a bite too."

"Oh. If you see her before I do will you let her know I'm looking for her?"

"Sure."

"Thanks."

I couldn't get to my office fast enough. There on my desk were the files I had given to Annie before leaving. Not a note or mark on them. Figures. She probably dumped them back on my desk as soon as I was out of sight. Though now that I think about what I saw, an affair would explain the flower vines. The real question here is do I pretend ignorance, or do I confront her with what I saw.

Not today. I can drop the files on Jim's desk and take my laptop home with me. That way I can avoid making a decision until tomorrow. With a quick word to my assistant Andy to rearrange a few phone calls, I'm off. First stop - Jim's office. Not even his assistant is at her post. It's silent as I place the files in the center of his desk. That's when I notice an odd paper sticking out of the side of his calendar. It's an ultrasound image. Dated three days ago.

"Oh no. No, no, no," this couldn't be happening. Either Annie is pregnant or Jim knocked someone up. Whichever it was I didn't want to be in the middle of it when it happened. I slid the picture back where it had been and was determined to get out of there as soon as I could. That's when I bumped into

Annie on the way back into her office.

"Good lunch?"

"Yeah - Lynn is pregnant. It's a baby whale tattoo." Smart me, way to bring up the one topic that may cause any number of issues.

"Aw that's super sweet. I wish I was a mom," it's not a denial of pregnancy but not a confirmation either.

"I just dropped those files on Jim's desk. I thought I'd finish out the day at home. The family is meeting for dinner tonight and it'll be faster for me to get there from home instead of the office." There, I've let her know I'm heading out. Now will she let me leave?

"Oh yeah, that makes lots of sense. I'll make sure that Jim looks them over. I'll send out a meeting invite so that we can all find a chance to talk about his idea. Have a good night," Annie gave my arm a gentle squeeze and went into her office.

Wishing I had less to carry so it wouldn't have been an issue to take the back stairs I waited for the elevator hoping I wouldn't run into Jim again. Finally, a bit of luck. I made it to the car park without running in to anyone that would question why I was leaving early. Once I was in my car and out of the parking lot I started going over what was in my fridge. After all there wasn't really a family dinner. That was just an excuse to get away from the office. Realizing that I had forgotten to pull anything out of the freezer for dinner meant a quick detour to the grocery store to pick up a half a dozen items I would need.

Some fancy cheese, a litre of milk and some noodles. A bottle of wine and some garlic bread. I could easily make some mac and cheese. That with garlic bread and wine would make a nice filling meal. I could do the research for Jim's idea after I cooked. Then I could curl up and watch a show. Thank goodness for tap. I was able to run through the register quickly once the cashier checked my ID for the wine. Back on the road home and I couldn't wait to crawl into some sweats and relax a little. A block away from my modest house and there were cars everywhere! Jamming the whole street. Looks like someone was having a party, or a funeral. You could never really be sure anymore. That's the thing about a skull tattoo. They just appear and it could be moments to weeks later that you die, but you will die.

I was able to pull into my driveway without hitting anyone's car. As I unlocked the door I looked back over my shoulder and my driveway was now blocked. Lucky to get home when I did. Inside my house was warm and cozy. Not a big house but perfect for me. There's a wraparound porch, then inside you can see nearly everything. A large old fashioned Russian style fireplace in the center of the room with my kitchen on the far side. The dining room is on the right of the entry and beyond that is the powder room and office. Next to those and the kitchen is the living room. To my immediate left is the hall closet and behind that is the only bedroom, with a huge bathroom and closet off it. There's a little laundry closet in the kitchen. Everything is done in soft pastel blues and white. The floor is a light gray wood looking tile. I love my home. It had taken a long time to get every detail right when I had it renovated. The contractor kept saying I should put in a staircase and go up – with more bedrooms the house would be worth more. I don't like people enough to want them to have a comfortable place to stay when they visit.

After dropping my computer on the coffee table and taking the groceries to the kitchen I popped into the bedroom to change. Once I was comfy, I got to work making an early dinner. All I could do was try to process what had happened. Even being logical wasn't working. How on Earth was I supposed to deal with Jim and Annie now? I know that in the end it's going to be my job to keep the company running regardless of what happens to them, but they are still both my friends. What I really need is the truth. Who was sleeping with whom first and whose baby is it? It's all just too much. At least I can say one good thing happened. I'm going to be an aunt.

With the mac and cheese in one oven and the garlic bread in the other it was time to pop open that bottle of wine. Which just brings up the issue with Jim's new tattoo. Annie was right he does have an issue with drinking and has had since we were in school. His drink of choice wasn't Kahlua though; he always went with whiskey or scotch of some kind. He was right, we could open a specialty shop that served alcoholic drinks. While I was waiting, I wandered over to my office and booted the computer there. Before I knew it the timer in the kitchen was pinging away letting me know the bread was ready, I'd managed to get far enough into the research to know that there were bars that severed coffee and tea drinks but not one that did so exclusively or with any real variety. I'd already begun putting the numbers together and it looked like Jim was right. It would be a huge market.

The garlic bread was a little dark, but the mac and cheese was perfect. After grabbing my plate I wandered over to the living room and popped the TV on. Sometimes I just need a little background noise to distract me while my brain thinks through the events of my day. That's when it occurred to me that I hadn't seen Jim with the usual signs of having had one too many in a few months. Usually when that happened he'd come in to work and the lights would be kept dimmed in and around his office, his secretary wouldn't let anyone but Annie or I through and she'd defer all his calls or arrange for a call back at a later date. Thinking back it had been about five months since that had happened. Obviously Annie thought he was still going overboard. The question is did she not notice because she wasn't around or because he wasn't around?

There was no way to look up an image of the man Annie had been with that day. I hadn't seen the name on the ultrasound image that Jim had either. All these thoughts just kept circling in my mind. I needed to find a way to be prepared when everything finally came to light. A divorce could destroy the company if not handled correctly. It would mean hiring some extra staff since I would have to take on some more duties. I didn't have much of a social life as it was, if things between Annie and Jim went south I wouldn't even get to see my family.

I needed to find time to set up a baby shower for Lynn as well. She said she wasn't going to tell mom and dad yet but I doubt she'll be able to keep it from them. Grandmothers tended to get the grandbaby's tattoo showing up in conjunction with the child that is having the baby. A jingle on a commercial caught my attention. It was a reminder that I needed to take some me time where I didn't think about work or family. Just take care of myself.

I flipped off the TV and took my

dishes to the kitchen. I should have put them in the dishwasher, but I didn't feel like dealing with them. There was always later. I had to let the food cool down before it went in the fridge so I could do them at that time. It was just starting to get dark outside and the street was still full of cars. As I watched, the door across the street opened and a man came wandering out, weaving a little. Probably drunk. He got into the car that was blocking my driveway and pulled away. A minute later a woman came flying out of the house and looked around in a panic. Looks like it was a skull party.

That's what we called them. When someone got a skull tattoo and stopped caring about their life. Often people would throw a party to cheer them up. Then the person would die in some silly accident and likely take others with them. I always felt that it was a self-fulfilling prophecy. Sometimes there's nothing you can do to save the person. Like with my brother. Mom lost the baby through no fault of her own. Or an elderly person whose heart simply gives out. Then there's the ones like the man that drove away. If he hadn't had the skull appear, then he wouldn't have had a party and driven drunk in the first place.

I needed to get some sleep. Tomorrow was going to be a long day. There wasn't much space in the fridge, but I was able to squeeze the leftovers into a dish and fit them in on the shelf. Once I tossed the dishes in the dishwasher I wandered around turning off lights and shut down my computer. It had gotten chilly in the house so I made a fire up in the fireplace. It would keep the house warm all night. That was the nice thing about having it, I didn't need to use my heat for most of the spring and fall. That done, I double checked the doors to make sure everything was locked and then went through the double French doors to my bedroom. I had a king-sized bed done in shades of blue. I curled up and even though it wasn't that late I fell asleep immediately.

1 Day before the skull appeared

I normally avoid the news but I had decided to check the local for if there were any road closures. It had snowed in the middle of the night. I could see the ice on my driveway. There was a

THE SKULL

list of closures for the ice and one for a bad car wreck. Looks like I was right about the guy from last night. They were saying it was a drunk who ran a red and caused a semi to jack knife into several other vehicles. There were a few survivors but not the drunk.

I had already grabbed breakfast and was just putting the dishes in the dishwasher when my phone went off. It was a text from Jim wanting to come past my house before work. I told him to come on over and shut off the TV. If it was that bad out I may just work from home. I didn't have any meetings that day and I could get Andy to forward any calls to my work cell. With my laptop already set up in my office it would be easier and safer just to stay home.

While I waited for Jim I sent out

messages to Annie and Andy that I was going to work from home. The knock on the door came sooner than I had expected. I let Jim in, normally he was dressed in formal clothes for work but today he was in jeans and a sweater. It was odd since he had said he would be heading to work after coming over.

"Thanks for letting me catch you before you head in. I want to talk to you about something personal. It may come as a bit of a shock, but I think you need to know everything that is going on. You may have noticed that Annie and I have been having problems for a while. Yesterday she moved out of the house. She's decided that we need to see a marriage counselor and if that doesn't help us find some common ground that we need to get divorced," Jim dropped on to my couch as he finished speaking. I was a little floored. I hadn't expected him to be the first one to tell me what was actually going on in their marriage. In the past he'd always avoided speaking about his relationship with Annie directly.

"Ok. I admit that I had noticed the two of you arguing more than normal. I will also admit that when I was in your office dropping paperwork on your desk yesterday that I saw an ultrasound image. Does that have anything to do with what is happening between you and Annie?" My back was getting straighter as I perched on the end of my couch facing Jim. I didn't want to be the one to bring it up but this was the only way to find out.

"Ah. Well, yes and no. You see about

THE SKULL

6 months ago after Annie and I got into that really big fight, I ended up going to a bar and having a little too much to drink. While I was there, I met a woman. She had just left her husband. From what she had said he'd been beating on her. Her name is Mary. I'm not sure if you knew but I keep an apartment down from the office so that when Annie and I fight I can go there and sleep. That night I offered Mary the second room. After a few days of her staying there we got to talking and I said I'd help her get a job and let her stay there rent free if she kept it clean. Once she got a job she was going to find a place of her own and would move out. I admit that one thing led to another. Annie doesn't want kids, you know that. I've always wanted to be a parent. One night, after another fight, I went to the apartment

and Mary was very sympathetic and things got… Well, you don't need the details. So, the answer to your unspoken question is yes, the baby is mine. I'm letting Mary stay at the apartment free so that it covers the cost of childcare. She will still work for food money and I will pay for things like clothes and toys for the baby. No Annie doesn't know about it yet. Please don't tell her, I need to do this the right way."

"Let me guess, the night you and Mary got together you were drinking Kahlua?"

"Yeah, we were. I still think that my idea for the specialty drinks is a good one though. I will probably have to give up my stake in the company – this would let me keep a portion that Annie wouldn't want."

"Alright. I can tell you that the numbers are looking good. You were right that there's no one doing what you want to do. However, I haven't finished looking at the cost output versus the possible inflow of money. There may be less interest in that than you may think."

"That's ok. If it works, then it works if not, then not. I'm ok with whatever you find out." Jim seemed less nervous now that the information was out. My phone pinged to let me know a message was in. Andy letting me know that Annie was on her way to my house.

"Thank you for letting me know what was happening. Annie is on her way here and I think it might be better if you were to head out before she arrives."

With a sigh Jim stood and went over to my door. The wet soaking through my socks let me know that he hadn't bothered taking off his boots before wandering through my house. I followed him out on to the porch where he swept me up in a big hug before giving me a kiss on the cheek and whispering his thanks for my not judging him for what was happening and his part in what happened.

"Just so you know you will always have a job as long as I am able to run a business. You're an amazing friend and I'm glad I can lean on you."

"Yeah, I'm glad you told me – it'll make getting the work done easier and you know I'm always around if you need me for anything. Drive safe."

The pool of water by my couch was

the first thing I cleaned up. I had my mop still in my hand when there was a knock on the door as a gust of cold air swept through the house.

"Hey – thanks for leaving the door unlocked for me." Annie's hair swirled around her shoulders as she came in. She wandered across and perched in the same spot Jim had used only a minute or two before.

"So, what's up?"

"Well, I wanted to talk to you about maybe crashing here for a couple nights. I left Jim last night. Until he admits his drinking issue and is willing to speak with a councilor I'm not going to go back. I just need a day or two to find a place for myself," she couldn't meet my eyes.

"Are those the only reasons or does

this have something to do with the guy I saw you making out with yesterday during your lunch?" immediate regret. I shouldn't have brought it up but Jim was being honest and Annie wasn't telling me everything.

"How?! Alright fine, I admit that a few months ago when Jim and I had that big blow out and he stormed out I couldn't be in the house. I went to the hotel spa – you remember the one where we got those amazing massages? Well, the spa was closed but I was able to get a room and I thought why not go have a nice dinner and a drink? No harm since I knew Jim would be drinking like crazy anyways. When I was sitting at the bar waiting for a table this guy came up to me and bought me a drink. A few drinks later and the waiter comes to seat me and since I was having a good time I thought 'Hey why not have a nice dinner with this guy?' He was funny and made me feel good."

"And?"

"And I know I shouldn't have but I had a good night. There I said it. I'm having an affair. I won't tell you his name because you're just going to judge me for this anyways and it would be better for him."

"Fine. The question I have for you then is why aren't you staying with him? What does he do for a living?"

"He's married. He'd had a business meeting and the client had left and he was celebrating that night. Needless to say, I can't stay with him. He's in the tech industry, some big shot. I don't know much else mostly because I don't care. I haven't bothered asking. After that fight Jim basically stopped wanting to be with me, we can't even have a civil conversation anymore. That's why I left. I don't want to stay at a hotel, I don't want anyone putting information out there that we've split since it would affect the company."

"You know my house only has the one bedroom? That means you'll have to sleep on the fold out, you can use the powder room at night and we can share the bath and shower in my room. Does that work for you?"

"Yeah, that'll work. I promise I will find a place as soon as possible. In fact let me go get my bag from the car and I will pull up rental listings right now. If I can arrange a place then I'll be out even sooner," she left the door wide open letting all the heat out while she went to the car.

I wasn't looking forward to her staying. Annie had always been a little selfish when it came to life. Not all trust fund kids are bad but she did have a bit of a mean streak when she was being called out for bad behavior. My home is my place of peace. Having someone – even a close friend – staying there is difficult at best. That's why I chose no second floor when remodeling. I started mopping all the water up all over again. By the time I got to the door Annie was back. Seeing me holding the mop she sat her stuff down and took a minute to kick her shoes off. Since it had gotten so chilly in my house I went over and added wood to the fire. I knew it wouldn't take too long for the house to heat up again.

True to her word after dumping her things all over the living room and powder room Annie pulled out her computer and began working on finding an apartment. I retreated to my bedroom. With the doors closed I took a couple deep breaths and tried to forget how I had hoped to get work done at home and not have to worry about seeing Jim or Annie today. How is it that I ended up with both of them coming past and neither of them living in their own home? I can only wish that Jim had volunteered to go live in his apartment when Annie decided to call it quits. I can't even say anything to Annie about going home since I'm not supposed to know about Jim's situation.

Some guy in the tech industry… I should ask my brother-in-law Mark.

Maybe they had crossed paths. With that thought I went and had a shower. A little peace and quiet will do wonders. As soon as the shower was on there was a banging on my door.

"When you're out come see what I've found!!! I think this place will be perfect! It's close to work and to my boyfriend's business too!"

Worst. Shower. Ever.

Every couple of minutes Annie would knock with another great find. Or a question. Or in need of an opinion. This is why there was no guest room and the fold out was lumpy and uncomfortable. I still don't know why I agreed to this. I cut my shower short and got dressed in soft comfy pants and a tank top with a cardigan of the same material and colour as the pants.

A soft emerald green. Looking through the doors from my bedroom there is Annie. Sprawled out on the sofa. Laptop sitting on her lap and a Victoria's Secret cart with more than a month's pay in it.

"Hey so did you find a place?"

"Yeah kinda. I found two. One is the perfect location but the other really calls to me. Here have a look."

The first apartment was in the perfect location. Even I had to admit that. Only a block from work. The building had her favorite restaurant in it and the hotel with the spa she loved was right across the street. The issue was the apartment itself. It was tiny. It was a studio with a post-it sized bathroom and only one closet. Not likely to work with the kind of wardrobe that Annie kept let alone the cart full of new additions. The second apartment was beautiful. Chef's kitchen, a dozen closets. A bedroom that looked like a fancy hotel. Huge spa style bathroom. Downside location. It was way too close to my place. Four blocks away. It meant I'd end up carpooling with her constantly whether I wanted to or not.

"Honestly, I would go for the one with the good location. I mean between hot married guy, the hotels, the restaurants, the spas, and work how much time are you really going to spend in the apartment? Or you keep the house and boot Jim out. Just a thought."

"I was thinking the first one too. It's just that it's so small. You're right though. I won't really be spending a ton of time there. I don't really cook;

with the restaurants so close I won't need too. I don't think I want to stay in the house. I am the one cheating. It really wouldn't be right for me to stay."

"Ok. Again, it was just a thought."

"I'll contact the person that's listed on the first place and see if it's still available. Want to go with me to view it?"

"Sure," anything I can do to convince her to not stay here.

When you have a person staying with you there's this feeling of obligation, like you have to keep the guest entertained. Even with long term friends. Once I'd agreed to go with her to the apartment she went back to online shopping. I pulled some food out of the freezer to thaw in time for lunch. Then I went into my office closed the doors and continued to work on Jim's idea.

*   *   *   *   *

"Hey, what have you got around here for lunch?"

"Oh, I pulled out some rabbit to thaw. I was going to make some rice; veggie stir fry and then fry up the meat."

"Oooo – that sounds delicious."

Annie popped a show on the TV and sat while I made our lunch. There should be enough for leftovers later, not that Annie would ever eat leftovers. Some things never changed. When Annie was a kid her family had a fresh meal every sitting and there were never repeated dishes during the week. When we met she didn't know what a leftover was and when she found out, Annie vowed never to eat food that was left over. According to Jim she had kept that promise. I thought it was ridiculous but when you grow up with money…

"Lunch is ready," Annie inevitably just lounged and expected me to serve her. Which I did since she's the guest.

"I heard back from that guy. We can go see the apartment the day after tomorrow. I don't know. Maybe I should contact the other place too just in case this one doesn't pan out."

"I'm sure you'll be fine and get the apartment downtown."

"Oh. I arranged for Jim and I to go to

marriage counselling tomorrow. So just as an FYI you'll be on your own."

"Are you going to tell him about the affair?"

"Maybe. I mean I should. I don't know. I don't want to hurt him and I know that this whole side thing doesn't really mean anything to me or the guy. He's never going to leave his wife. I know that. It's just until Jim deals with his own issues – like his drinking – I don't want to say anything."

"He's going to find out. That's one of the things that the councilor will insist on – complete honesty and all issues being aired."

"I know," she did her best to give me a hang dog expression. I wasn't having any of it. Annie had done this in school too. When she didn't study for something she also wouldn't take responsibility when she flunked. There'd be a dozen other reasons for her to not study for the test. Then she'd use either her beauty or perfectly contrived sadness to manipulate a retest or a perfect score.

The rest of the day was spent reassuring Annie that she was right to get that apartment. I managed to flesh out the numbers for Jim and sent him a message with the information and the suggestion that he put together a presentation for Annie to convince her that the project should go through.

The day of appearance.

Annie was up at the crack of dawn

getting ready for the day. I had about 10 minutes in the bathroom to get ready before she was standing at the front door complaining that I was taking too long.

"We don't have to carpool. You're parked behind me," even with the obvious being stated Annie wouldn't leave until I was in her car. It meant that when she felt like leaving work I'd either have to go with her or get a cab.

The drive was one of the scariest of my life. Instead of focusing on her driving she was busy drinking coffee with one hand and texting her boyfriend with the other while using her knees to drive. If she had gotten into an accident it wouldn't have been her first. It wouldn't have even been the first one with me in the passenger seat. Once we were parked and I could finally stand up we went up to our offices. Jim was in before us. He flagged me from his door, as I sat in front of him I took the time to really look at Jim.

He was looking much healthier than even when we were in college. He'd always had a slightly grey look to his face, small bags under his eyes and had always been an untidy mess. Even in a suit he had looked a little sloppy. Now he looked entirely different. The grey was gone along with the bags. He was neat and fresh, and he seemed more alive than he ever had been. Maybe this new woman and the baby on the way was better for him than his marriage to Annie. It still wasn't going to make my life any easier when they eventually split…

"So how did the research turn out?"

"Really well. You're on to something. I've gone ahead and come up with some sample ideas. I've put together a small presentation for you to go over and make your own – it should be in your email along with all the numbers you'll need. If I can make a suggestion, I would come up with a couple of those specialty drinks and then serve them during the presentation to Annie. She's not likely to turn one down."

"You're the best! I have a couple recipes that I've been experimenting with and I think they will work. I have a dozen more that I'm going to flesh out after I get these ones down. Would you arrange to meet with Annie about this say, the day after tomorrow? It'll give me a chance to finish everything up and have the drink ingredients on hand…"

"Sure thing Jim. I'll go do that now. Oh and just as an FYI I need to go down to the warehouse in a couple hours since it's inventory day. I'll probably be there the rest of my day. Just in case you need me. I'm having Andy deal with my calls and may not hear my cell."

"No worries. Enjoy inventory day," this was a long running joke between Jim and I. When the business first started and it was just the three of us getting everything set up we were supposed to go over the inventory together but inevitably Annie had other things to do that allowed her to disappear for the whole day and Jim kept sneaking sips from a flask he had in his pocket. He fell asleep when we were about a quarter of the way through. Once I had completed the inventory basically on my own, I decided to be juvenile and drew on his face with a pen. Across his forehead I wrote 'I can't hold my coffee' then took several pictures and sent them to Annie. Oddly enough she didn't think it was funny but when he finally woke up and saw what I had done he thought it was hilarious.

It's been a rare occasion when someone else appreciates my very twisted and warped sense of humor. Annie had never found the jokes I made funny. Jim only rarely did, though I think he often hid how he felt because he knew that Annie would disapprove of such humor. All these thoughts rolled through my head as I went down to the bottom floor. The back half of the building served as the company warehouse. It also held the employee entrance. The only people with assigned parking spots are the owners. Everyone else either came in early to get one of the few spots in the tiny lot or had to park in the structure across the street. Most of the time I beat everyone but the earliest of the warehouse crews in to work so I usually had a spot in the lot. It made sneaking out easier in some ways. Being able to park close meant I could 'pop out' for something and with all the product stacked up on the shelving if you walked through the back isle down to the end and then took a left you could slip out and not be stopped.

The problem was that if you had worked there long enough you knew what routes I used to avoid being noticed and then you could easily corner me. At least on inventory day I got to sit in the foreman's office and just go over the numbers as they came in. We usually got done early and sent everyone home. Even the store front closed early on inventory days. They were in the other section of the bottom floor. As long as no one had decided to steal anything it should be ok.

Garry was the foreman on duty during inventory. A large man with dark skin a smooth head and a deep laugh. He sported a goatee and was sensibly dressed for his job in a work shirt and pants in the company colours of navy blue and white. He already had drinks set up and all the inventory records set out for the day.

"There's the lady I've been waiting on. Your drink is still nice and hot – so far everything is matching the records.

Shall I pull out the cards?" It was tradition. We would sit and play rounds of gin rummy with our favorite drinks until everything was done. Then I'd sneak out early…

Which is when I realized that Annie had forced me to come to work with her. She and Jim had counselling this afternoon. Unless I caught a cab or found a lift, I wasn't going to get home until Annie felt like going there. Which with the way she had been behaving meant I wasn't going home with her anytime soon.

"How far in are we?" I began to shuffle the cards. I wasn't as good as a professional but card games when I was a child were one of the main stays at home.

"About halfway through. It should

only take a couple more hours. I told the night crew they could come in late or leave early tomorrow if they started the inventory this morning for us. They did their fair share and earned the extra time off paid."

"Agreed. It means the rest of us can go home early too. After all it won't be until tomorrow morning that processing starts again for the orders and shops. I'll be sure to let payroll know about our decision."

The next few hours were spent relaxing and playing cards. The inventory was done only three hours later. I still had more than half a day free. I didn't want to be in the office when everything came out between Annie and Jim. I didn't want to be at home when Annie came back either. Since I was smart enough to have brought all my things down to Garry's office I walked over to my favorite restaurant and picked up two to go orders of fish and chips before ordering an Uber over to my sisters' house. With the pregnancy she should be having cravings for food she normally wouldn't have eaten. Her house was within walking distance to mine so when I was done I could just wander home and enjoy the sunlight for a change. Lynn's house was huge. Three floors, the bottom where you walk in was just for entertaining guests. It was dominated by a large chef's kitchen which was open to the living and dining areas. On one side of the entry was a hallway that leads to the guest rooms. All of which were large and had their own en suites and walk-in wardrobes. The second floor was set up as the family living area with the top floor as the family bedrooms. I rarely saw the second floor. The chef's kitchen was always well stocked.

Lynn had given me the key ages ago – I don't think Mark knew. I let myself in and set the food up on the counter when I heard some muffled noises coming from the direction of the guest rooms. Intense worry gripped me, what if it was Lynn and she was having a problem with the baby? I had no idea I could move so fast when I opened the door to the guest room all I caught was a glimpse of naked bodies and blankets flung everywhere. I quickly and quietly closed the door. Well, I guess Lynn and Mark were still feeling romantic.

I made sure the food was covered before leaving a note telling Lynn to

THE SKULL

enjoy dinner with Mark. I walked home considering ordering in since I didn't get the meal I'd planned. It should be hours before Jim or Annie started looking for me. The pain in my left arm hit suddenly and was so intense I hit my knees. After several seconds it began to ease. It took several more minutes for my eyes to stop watering long enough to see. A new tattoo for me was unusual. I had my life fairly well planned out. When a tattoo arrived it was normally just confirmation that I was on the right track. I rolled up my sleeve to see what had changed so drastically.

There staring back up at me was a skull.

2 PANIC

I couldn't stand up. A skull. My days were now numbered. I hadn't done anything that could cause my own death. It must be something like food poisoning or a car accident that would take me. I could only hope that it would be weeks or months before it happened. One thing was for sure: I couldn't wear short sleeves. I couldn't let anyone know that a skull had appeared. I needed to go through my days as if nothing was wrong. That meant getting up off the cold cement and going home. Now. One foot at a time. Slow deep breaths. Watch at every crosswalk to make sure I'm ok and not going to get hit.

As I walked, I continued an inner monologue to keep myself calm. It was difficult to focus. There was a part of me that just wanted to tell everyone in my life, have a skull party and then let the world do its worst. It was a small part that wanted to give up and give in, but it was also very loud. The idea of fighting what everyone would say was inevitable seemed so daunting. Deep down I knew I had to fight though. I needed to see Lynn's little whale come into the world. I needed to be part of his or her life.

By the time I got home I had conquered my fear. I was burningly angry. Why me? Why was this happening to me? It just wasn't fair! After an hour of pacing around the house I had managed to calm down enough to think clearly. All I needed to do was figure out how I was going to die and when so that I could avoid what was coming to get me. After all, if I didn't let the skull dictate everything I thought and did then who's to say I would really die?

I just needed to create a plan. Sure enough, when I really needed it, my mind was blank. I sat down and took a deep breath. I could pull myself together and get through this. The light was fading when I came back to myself – I had sat there for most of the day just staring into space. Slowly I got up and promptly almost fell onto my face as pins and needles began through my legs. A quick shower and some pjs then it was just a matter of food. I blindly opened an app and ordered the first thing from the first restaurant on the list. At this point it didn't matter what I ate. As I got through the numbness that had settled over me again it was like my mind started to go into overdrive. I began to clean the house, I double checked to make sure I was wearing a long-sleeved shirt, I checked my cell for messages. Nothing from any of the family – which was odd since I had left that note for Lynn and she was usually good at thanking me for little surprises. A text from Annie saying she was staying out for the night and reminding me that I was meeting her first thing in the morning at the apartment she was going to look at.

That was one thing that had gone my way. With no Annie tonight I could lose my hold on my emotions as much as I liked so long as I met her in the morning. There'd be no questions.

The last message was from Jim. He was asking if I knew where Annie had gone – apparently she hadn't shown up for their counselling session. That had been hours ago. I sent him a text back apologizing and letting him know that I hadn't seen her since that morning and that I didn't know where she was now. Since it was unlikely that I'd hear from anyone else today, I checked to see where my food was. According to the tracker it was nearly at my house. I dug out my debit card and waited for the tell-tale knock on the door. After I had paid I sat with my food eating, but not tasting it. I was still numb in some ways. An early night for me. I lay in my bed, staring at the ceiling, sleep evading me. Going over my day again and again.

At some point I passed out. When I woke the sun was up and my phone was ringing.

"Where the hell have you been?!?!?" Annie's voice was hitting the point where she was screeching.

"Sorry I had a long day with inventory yesterday and forgot to put my alarm on," I felt terribly groggy and my arm was still sore.

"Well you missed me getting that apartment. I'm coming past and picking up my stuff. I already have the key and I've been shopping all morning for furniture. It's being delivered this afternoon," Annie continued to talk for several more minutes with no real point. Apparently I was going to love the colours she had picked for her bedding.

When she finally got off the line I got up and realized it was Saturday. At least I had a couple days to relax. Annie got to my place sooner than I'd hoped. I hadn't eaten breakfast yet. She kept up a running commentary as she gathered her things.

"I mean really the session was awful. He didn't even hear me when I told him I was seeing someone else. Jim just kept droning on and on about how he isn't an alcoholic and didn't need help. I think I'm dodging a bullet by moving out now."

"Huh. That's odd."

"What?"

"According to the text I got from Jim he was looking everywhere for you. He said you never showed to the session," Annie cast a look of pure contempt at me.

"Really? You're going to listen to the drunk over your best friend?"

"No, of course not, it's just that is what he sent me. How drunk do you think he was? Enough that he couldn't remember going to counselling?"

"Yeah, he was pretty blasted. I wouldn't put it past him to have gone straight to a bar after the meeting too. Anyways I've got to run. The furniture should be there in about 40 minutes and I need to let them in. You can come over tonight and help me set everything up," Annie swished her way out of my house leaving shoe prints all over my floor.

I didn't believe anything she said. I knew Jim wasn't drinking which means she had lied about being at the meeting and telling him that she was cheating. I didn't want to be in the middle of anything, but I felt I needed to let Jim know that she had moved out and what she had told me about the session. The call couldn't have gone worse. Jim was devastated to hear that Annie had moved into her own place. He made the decision to take his girlfriend and move back into the house. After all it was a waste of money that he would be needing to keep paying for the apartment while leaving a house completely empty. He promised not to let Annie know I'd said anything.

With every day that passed Annie had

become less and less a friend that deserved my trust. Still, I had known her forever, I could give her a second chance. It was probably just the bad influence of her boyfriend. I'd be there when the relationship inevitably ended – after all it couldn't last if he was married too. One of them wouldn't be willing to leave their spouse and since Annie was already split from Jim it meant the boyfriend was the one who would try to have it all.

I started mopping up all the prints Annie had left on my floor, then I put on the laundry with all the bedding she had used. There was still more to clean. At least it kept my mind off the pain in my arm. Quiet introspection had never been comfortable for me even with my deep-set desire to be alone. The skull circled my mind. I didn't care what else needed to be done. I had to get out and away from everything. It took a little digging but I found my picnic basket. I went through the cupboards and fridge tossing random foods in, followed by my favorite outdoor blanket.

It was a bit of a drive to the outskirts of town. There was a lake there that was always overly busy during the summer but this early in the spring was quiet in the picnic areas. The trees had just come out in leaves, there were some flower buds on them. The lake shimmered in the light. The breeze was a little on the too cold side. I pulled my cardigan closer. I was going to miss this. If you could miss things when you die.

There had to be something more beyond what we saw. Where could the tattoos come from if there was just nothing? The sound of a bug buzzing by my ear caught my attention. There was a small pain – a little early for mosquitos but I suppose it was possible. I reached up and flicked the air around my ear before touching the bite. My hand came away with blood on it. The bite felt more like a cut. It was odd. With a sigh I stood and went down to the water. I rinsed the blood off my hand and wiped away as much as I could from my ear. As I turned around I caught a movement behind me. A man standing there looking confused as if he wasn't expecting me to be standing there.

He was dressed in jeans and a dark shirt; he was tall with dark hair and grey eyes. With a slight shift on his feet, he began to bring his hand up.

Which is when I saw the gun. I threw myself backwards into the water as I took a deep breath. I may be small but I'm a good swimmer. I didn't need to go too far offshore to be deep enough to turn and swim parallel to the shoreline. I knew there was a boat launch south of the picnic area. My father had been so excited the first time he'd launched his new boat from there. Mom hadn't been as happy – she'd been hoping he'd spend more time at home when he retired. Funny the things that come through your mind when you think you're going to die. I felt oddly calm. Detached from everything. Like nothing really mattered anymore.

None of this was part of my plan.

3 WHAT NOW?

I was freezing by the time I got to the boat launch. I didn't want to go on shore right away in case the guy had managed to follow my progress. There had been shots hitting the water when I had turned south but they had stopped after a couple minutes swimming. There was a large patch of forest between the launch and the picnic areas. It had likely been too thick for him to get a clear shot at the water. If I needed I could always swim up to that area.

Slowly I raised myself out of the water. I could see a car backing up to the launch with a boat. It was at a poor angle. They were going to need to pull back up and straighten out before bringing the boat down again. There was a woman with her kids trying to give directions to the person in the car. I couldn't see if it was a man or a woman in there. Looking around there was no sign of the man who had tried to kill me. With that reassurance I swam up towards the launch wading back in once my feet hit the ground. I couldn't really feel them anymore. Just the weight of my body being supported.

The wind picked up and I felt like ice everywhere. Thousands of little knives pricking me all over. The look on the woman's face as one of her kids pointed at me was all I needed to know that I looked like I had drowned. Maybe this was how it happens. Not with drowning but with the hypothermia that likely will take me before I can warm up. I had made it nearly all the way out of the water when things went dark.

A bright light shining in my eyes is what brought me awake. I still felt freezing in my limbs, but my chest felt warm. As the light moved away a face took its place. Sound was slowly coming back to me as well.

"Miss, can you hear me?" A paramedic, that's who was leaning over me. I could hear the siren in the background. I must be on my way to the hospital.

"Yes, I can hear you. My chest feels warm, but my arms and legs are freezing! Oh, my ear! That guy shot at me and caught my ear!" On reflection, when you're that cold your thought processes must slow down. I know I wasn't making much sense at all. The look of confused sympathy on the paramedic's face was enough to tell me that.

"Miss, you have hypothermia. We've got warm packs around your chest. The fact that you can feel your limbs is good. You may still lose a finger or toe but it's a good sign that you can feel your arms and legs. Chances go down when that happens. As for your ear – there's a little cut. Probably got it when you were in the water. I must say if you were going to kill yourself this was probably the least efficient way. I know it's a tough one when a skull appears, but you should think about how your family will feel before you try anything else."

"No, I wasn't trying to kill myself. A guy was shooting at me and I dove into the water to get away. He was a terrible shot," I don't know why convincing this man was so important but in that moment it was. I needed help. Hospital staff and medics are required to report shootings. It would involve the police and hopefully get me a little protection.

"We are only a couple minutes from the hospital and then the doctors will take over," the medic seemed displeased that I had stuck to the truth. The rest of the ride was in relative silence, other than the siren.

There was a flurry of motion when we arrived. I was taken into the back and placed on to a warm bed with lots and lots of blankets. I was hooked up to a bunch of monitors and an IV. I couldn't hear everything that the paramedics said to the doctor, but I did see the one who had been in the back of the ambulance with me touch his left forearm. Right where my skull was. There was a look of pity on the doctor's face for a moment before he went back to the professional look that all doctors put on when dealing with severe trauma.

The doctor issued a bunch of orders to nurses and interns for what seemed like forever before he turned to speak with me directly. By then all the people for the most part had filtered out of my little cubicle.

"Well suicide by drowning is not the best way to go since it rarely works out," somehow, he had managed a look of sternness and concern all at once.

"I didn't try to commit suicide. I was being shot at. The only direction I could go that would get me any kind of safety was the water. So I swam from the picnic area down to the boat launch and got help."

"Since you seem to be insisting on this I will have to let you know that I must inform the police of any shootings. Do you really want them to come here?"

"Yes."

"Alright then I will let them know."

After that he left and the nurses kept coming and checking my progress.

There was a lot of pain as I warmed up. Slowly my fingers and toes began to hurt. I knew I had been lucky this time, I wasn't going to lose a limb. I was still puzzled by the guy though. I hadn't done anything differently in my life, hadn't seen anything that could have caused someone to want to kill me. So why suddenly do I get a tattoo and hit man all at once?

The police appeared once the nurses began to remove the extra blankets. It looked like one of them had already spoken with the doctor. His face was set in sad lines. Like he'd seen one too many skull cases in his life. The other was much younger and seemed like he was willing to hear my story and just maybe do something about it.

"I'm Officer Andrews and this is my partner Officer Dutch. I understand there was an issue you wanted to speak with us about?" His sadness seemed to deepen the lines around his green eyes even more.

"Yes, the reason I ended up in that water was because a guy was shooting at me. You can go to the park and check. I'm sure there's evidence there. I was in the picnic area. My car should still be there as well. I need some kind of protection. This is not my imagination. This is reality," no matter what I said Andrews seemed to have already made his mind up. Dutch though kept shooting looks between me and his partner. It seemed like he wanted to go and check it out – even if it proved me a liar.

"Tell you what, Dutch and I will go take a look for you. However if we don't find anything then you have to allow the doctor to submit you for a psychiatric examine. That way everyone gets the help they need."

It was a huge risk since I couldn't be sure they would even bother looking but it was one worth taking, "Alright, that's fine. As long as you go and look. I want to be present so that I can show you where he was standing and what happened."

"We can't stop you from doing that. The doctor will have to discharge you first though."

He was right. I would have to wait until I was discharged to go with them. Still, it was a better bet than hoping that Andrews wouldn't force Dutch to not really look at the scene since I was just another crazy skull case. It was dark by the time I was discharged and that under great protest by the doctor who had wanted me to go straight from the emergency room to the psych floor.

I got in the car with the officers and they drove us all the way out to the park. Andrews was not wanting to bother but Dutch seemed like he was happy to be doing anything at this point. I got the feeling that Andrews tended to do the bare minimum and in doing so overlooked vital information. It was the same kind of thing that Annie did, and it drove me up the wall.

My picnic stuff was all still there. Surprisingly even my keys and wallet which I had tossed into the bottom of my basket were still there. It must have been too cold for people to care about stealing stuff from a park. The guy who had shot at me obviously wasn't trying to steal my things, which again brought the question of why to my mind.

After sitting down on the blanket where I had been only hours before I moved down to the water like I had explaining that I thought I'd had a bug bite and went to look at my reflection. Then turning and pointing out where I'd seen the man and how he had seemed surprised to see me by the water. It was all still so fuzzy that all I could remember of his features were the brown hair and grey eyes. Andrews just stood there listening maybe starting to believe I wasn't crazy.

Dutch pulled out his flashlight and started working his way away from us back to where I'd pointed and a then a little further over the hill until just the top of his head was visible to us.

"I've got something here," Andrews looked shocked and gestured for me to stay put while he went to check out what Dutch had found. Shortly after that a bunch of police vehicles started showing up and taping off the area.

"Miss, it seems you were right about the shooter. He was definitely here, and likely he took the shot at you cause you had messed up his plans. See, there's a dead body back there. My guess is he was going to drag it to the water and dump it in. Instead, he walked smack into you. We will need to put you in to police protection for the time being," although not at all apologetic for his earlier judgments Andrews was taking everything very seriously now.

"That's fine. I would like to gather my things and take my car home. Is that possible?"

"Yes ma'am – Officer Dutch will escort you and stay outside your house until we can make the arrangements. As soon as we have any information, we will let you know."

I quickly gathered up all my things and went to my car. Dutch checked it over before I was allowed in – just in case – then I drove home. I was starving and exhausted. With the officer wandering around the outside of my house I went and took a warm shower, set a fire in the fireplace and turned on some music. I stood in front of the open fridge door not really seeing the food. I closed the door and slid to the floor, my face in my shaking hands.

The events of the day were finally catching up with me. Had I managed to evade death? Does this mean I don't have to worry? No, of course not. That incident wouldn't have happened if I hadn't had the skull appear. Still, it goes back to the drunk from the skull party the other day. Was it the drinking too much at the party that led to his death or was he destined to die anyways from something else?

The only way to really know was to survive. That was looking harder and harder at this rate. A few deep breaths later and I had managed to pull myself together. I was still starving. I opened the fridge and reached in blindly pulling out food. I heated up the leftovers and ate them without tasting them. Put the dishes into the dishwasher and off with the music. I wasn't hearing it anyways. I hadn't put on my pajamas yet since I still had

Dutch lurking around outside. I should probably check on him or invite him in to sit until he heard back about my protection.

I walk over to the door and realize how late it really is, midnight already. There was silence out there. I could see the police car still parked in my driveway but there was no one in it. Dutch must be checking the perimeter. It must be boring sitting looking at a house with one person in it while waiting for orders. I could hear a siren a little way away. It seemed like it was heading in my direction. A click behind me followed by a gust of cold air let me know my back door had just been used.

Without thinking I opened the front and closed it behind me. I dove towards the police car and locked myself inside. I could see a foot on the far side of my porch peeking out from around the corner and a dark shadow passing in front of the windows. If I was careful whoever it was wouldn't see me in the car. I'm small enough to scrunch down and be little more than a shadow myself. The sirens were getting louder. Dutch must have called for help. The front door opened sending a splash of light across the porch and into the yard. There was a glimpse of the person before I ducked down hoping he hadn't seen me.

I could hear the cursing he was doing. It got louder before getting quieter again. The hair was standing up on the back of my neck. All my senses were screaming at me to get out of the car and run. Flashing lights across my hand caught my attention. Taking the risk, I popped my head up to see what was happening in my yard. There was a new police car sitting at the edge of the sidewalk and three cops had gotten out. Andrews was running up to the house calling out for Dutch. The other two cops were checking the area. I carefully opened the door of the car and they both whirled in my direction. I kept my hands up and visible.

"Officer Andrews, is Dutch ok?" I could hear the quaver in my voice as the guns that had been leveled at me began to slowly point down towards the ground.

"He's got a nasty bump on the head – if he hadn't been on the phone with me at the time I think things could have been a lot worse. What happened here?"

"I had a shower and something to eat. Watched a little TV. I came to the door to invite Dutch to sit inside since it's still cold at night and felt my back door open. I stepped outside and bolted for the car. I figured I could hide there and hopefully the guy that was there wouldn't see me. It was close, I could hear him cussing as he came across the front yard then it went quiet, and you showed up."

"We've got an ambulance on the way for Dutch, we'll take care of the lady from here Andrews. You go with your partner and let us know how he does."

"Thanks Jimmy," Andrews was squatting down next to Dutch and kept checking his wrist.

After Andrews and Dutch left with the ambulance the other officers came up to the house and began questioning me over and over about how the man had gotten in. I knew that I had locked that door. I never normally leave anything unlocked. And if I lose my key the spare is over at Lynn's which is a short walk so, I don't have one left outside where someone could find it.

There was only one conclusion – someone gave him the key to my place. I couldn't believe it though. There had to be some other way. Maybe he got my key copied while I was in the hospital. They had just been left lying in the basket for hours and hours. It would explain why he hadn't hidden that dead body when he'd clearly had the time. Eventually a crime scene team showed up and started dusting for prints. I was going to have to clean again.

Slowly people filtered out. There were two units parked out front and occasionally, two officers would get out and walk around the property. I closed the drapes and went to bed. At least it was Sunday now and I didn't have work. I glanced at my cell phone. There were dozens of missed calls from Annie, Jim, and Lynn. I couldn't deal with all of that right now. I was so tired I felt numb. I crawled into bed and went to sleep.

* * * * *

The banging on my door woke me. Lynn and Mark were standing there with one of the officers from out front next to them. I popped the door open and stood staring at the scene in front of me. Lynn was clearly upset, and Mark looked irritated. The officer was standing just off to one side staring at Mark like he suspected him of committing some horrible crime.

"Oh! Thank goodness you're ok! You didn't answer any of my calls and after I saw the news!" Lynn pushed into the house and wrapped me in her arms. It felt more like she wanted to wrestle than hug me. Mark stepped in and carefully took off his shoes. Once that was done, he wandered over to the living room and sat down. It took Lynn another ten minutes and a bout of tears before she let me go. "What on earth were you doing at the park having picnic anyways?"

"Honestly, I just wanted to go somewhere quiet to think. Somewhere outside. It was nice. The spot was mostly sheltered from the wind. I was enjoying the day until that guy showed up."

"You're lucky to be alive! The hospital called me you know. I'm your emergency contact! You didn't even wait for me to show up so that I could bring you home. Staying the night here was crazy – you should have come over to our place and stayed with us!"

"Lynn, I know you're upset but I was physically cleared to leave the hospital. The officers wanted me to show them where the guy had shot at me from in the park. I went there and did what I was supposed to do. They gave me police protection. Oh, and just to cap it all off I didn't put you in danger by being with you when that killer showed up looking for me last night. So maybe take a breath and relax a little, I'm ok."

"Are you really? I can see your new tattoo," Mark's quiet and steady voice broke through our traditional sister spat. Damn. I forgot to grab a cardigan to go over my sleep top. Lynn looked at Mark confused until he pointed at my arm. Her face went paler than my walls. She looked on the verge of fainting.

"Just calm down. I have managed to avoid getting killed twice already. I'm not going to give in and believe my time is limited. You know what I think about the tattoos not dictating our fates. I can't live with the idea that some silly mark is going to force me down a particular path."

Lynn burst into tears. Nothing Mark or I did seemed to calm her down.

Eventually Mark just gestured that he was taking her home and the two of them left. At least that was over with. I knew my parents wouldn't have found out yet since they don't watch the news and Lynn would never tell them to avoid upsetting them. That just left the messages from Annie and Jim. I went back to my bedroom and laid down. Grabbing my phone, I checked to see what had been sent to me over the last day.

The messages from Annie were frustrating. All of them were about what a terrible friend I was being since I hadn't shown up to help her with the furniture and was obviously ignoring her calls and texts.

Jim was a different kettle of fish altogether. At first there were the standard have a good weekend messages. Followed by an invitation to come over tonight to meet his girlfriend. Would I be the godmother for his new baby. Then a lot of concern since I wasn't answering him. A message saying he had come past to check on me, but I didn't come to the door and to please call and let him know I was ok. After some thought I decided to call Annie and get that over with first.

"Hey Annie. I'm sorry that I didn't answer – I was at the hospital and didn't have my stuff on me."

"Why would you go to the hospital? There's nothing wrong with you. Really you need to not be so dramatic about getting sick. You always do this – go a little crazy over a small cough. Well, you may come over and see my apartment next weekend. I have my man coming over in a little while and I don't need you showing up in the middle of everything."

"Ok that sounds good. I'll see you at work tomorrow." I'm not even sure she heard me. I think she hung up before I had finished speaking. Annie tends to do that to punish people when she's angry. Childish but something she has never been able to stop herself from doing. Next was Jim.

"Are you ok?" Not even a hello. He must have been waiting with the phone in his hand.

"At the moment yes. It's a long story."

"I don't care how long, I'm listening." So I told him everything. From dropping food off at Lynn's to the tattoo appearing and all the problems after that. He didn't interrupt me once.

"If you need to crash somewhere more secure you can come and stay with me. The house has the best security money can buy. I can hire some extra security guards. You know there's nothing I wouldn't do to keep you safe."

"That's very sweet Jim but I don't want to put you or your lady in harm's way. Especially not with a new baby coming. I'll be ok here."

"Ok – that's your choice. I'm coming over. You're not doing this alone." He hung up before I could say no. A half hour later Jim was on my doorstep with a bag of his stuff and an even bigger bag of food.

"I figured you probably hadn't thought about eating much since yesterday. You need to keep your energy up."

"What're we having?" I couldn't help

but giggle about the energy thing – it was something we had always done when getting ready to study for a test. Annie would be ridiculously late so Jim and I would always stuff ourselves with food before she showed up. When we did get food while she was present it always had to be healthy salads and such. She hasn't changed that much.

"I stopped past our favorite place and got loads of chicken tenders, fries, and best of all cakes for dessert. I think I bought enough to feed us both for a couple days," his smile turned in to a laugh as he admitted how much he'd bought.

"Honestly, I'm glad you did. It smells so good! You're right I haven't thought about eating. Last night I tried to pick something and ended up on the floor crying for a while then ate something from the fridge. I'm just glad that it wasn't outdated."

"So, what's your security system like?"

"Well, there's some cops sitting in cars out front. No doubt you met them as you came in. Other than that, there's a couple sturdy locks on the doors. I'm having them rekeyed since it seems the guy used a spare that I didn't know was out there. The locksmith should be here soon. Other than that, just my own senses. So far, they've been pretty dead on."

"Are you insane?" I could hear the edge in Jim's voice that says he's going to start yelling if I give him any kind of smart-ass answers.

"No. I live in a safe neighborhood. This is something out of the ordinary.

Until now the locks have been enough."

"Ok. We are getting you a proper security system. I know a guy. I don't want any arguments about this. You're too important to me and to just let you not be protected will drive me nuts. Also, I'm staying until this is over. I know you don't like guests, but I don't want an argument about that either," the look on Jim's face said that he had made up his mind. I would just have to live with it for a little while until the cops caught the guy. Then I could have my house back.

"Fine, but just so you know – the couch is lumpy, and I plan on using most of the hot water in the morning before work."

"Deal," with a smile Jim unpacked the

food then wandered into the office to call the security guy.

I sat on my couch nibbling at the food. I was hungry but I had no drive to eat. The sun was pouring in the windows, but it was cold out there. That's the problem with spring. You want to be outside when it's sunny and feels like it should be warm it turns out to still be cold.

Silly thought given that I was probably being hunted even now. Who knows where this guy may pop up next. With my luck it'd be when I was in the bath. A knock on the door alerted me to the arrival of the locksmith. Both doors were rekeyed in a short time and several copies were handed over to me. I immediately gave one to Jim. That way he could come and go as he pleased. The others I tucked away with a reminder to give one to Lynn when I saw her next. I couldn't seem to concentrate after that. Jim's guy showed up with all kinds of high-tech equipment. I agreed to allow cameras on the outside of the house but not the inside. Jim seemed disappointed but I stood firm on that. Motion sensors and sensors on all the windows and doors. Three control pads, one by each door and one wired in next to my bed so that I could switch it all on from the comfort of my room.

While it was all being installed, I did my best to stay out of the way. There was an old movie on TV called Arsenic and Old Lace. It was a favorite of my mother's back when I was a kid. She had a thing for Cary Grant. I sat and watched the antics of the aunts for a while unmoving and able to forget the world. It was the best day I'd had in a while. Just as Cary Grant was running up the stairs with his bride yelling "Charge" Jim plunked down next to me on the couch and tossed an arm along the back.

"I made the code your mother's birthday. Month then day. I hope that was ok. If not, I can help you change it."

"No that's fine. Though I'm a little surprised you remember her birthdate. You always have trouble remembering Annie's and your anniversary not to mention her birthdate."

"To be candid I never forgot them, I just didn't feel like celebrating a marriage that has never seemed to really work and Annie always hated the few times I tried to do nice things for her birthday, so I left it to her to decide what she wanted. I'm sorry that she usually dumps that job on you."

"She always gives me a list of what she wants and how many guests and so on. It's not that much work other than finding someone who can do the cake." Jim gently tugged on one of my curls to get me to look at him.

"I know that when the divorce goes through things are going to be tough on you. Annie will probably demand full loyalty to her and only her. Which is going to make things hard for us since we will still be friends. I don't want to give up our friendship, but I'd understand if you wanted me to back off. It's ok to say it."

"Yeah, it will be tough when the divorce goes through. Mostly for the company. Annie is so involved in her own drama she can't see what's happening around her. This morning I called her back since I didn't answer her yesterday and instead of asking why, she lectured me on how I'm too dramatic. How every little cough sends me in to the hospital. That I'm not a good friend because I didn't come over and help set up her furniture for her. At this point I'm not even sure I want to be friends with her at all anymore." Even though it had been picking at the back of my brain all day I still began to cry. Jim lifted me onto his lap and cuddled me close to him. He didn't try to tell me to stop. He just let me cry all over him.

When I finally wound down, I just leaned my head on his shoulder. Jim reached over to the side table and handed me some Kleenex. We sat in silence while commercials played on the TV. After a while I scooted back to the couch but continued to lean into his side.

"You didn't answer my messages from yesterday. Will you be my baby's godmother?"

"I'd love to. Though I would like to meet your girlfriend before that is decided."

"Of course. When all this crazy is over and you're feeling better about life we can all have dinner together."

"That sounds like a plan."

We spent the rest of the day in pleasant silence watching old movies and eating chicken. When it got dark Jim set up the pullout and I got the bedding for him. Once he was settled, I went into my room and crawled into my bed.

It was the odd sound coming from the living room that woke me in the middle of the night. I couldn't have had more than three or four hours of sleep when the thumping started. I sat up and looked through the doors, but the fireplace was blocking my view. Quietly I got up and crept around to the kitchen – I didn't want to wake Jim if it had just been him turning over.

Sure enough Jim was wide awake. Every time he turned over his feet would catch the coffee table and then he'd start to quietly cuss. I stood there watching for a while, after the fourth or fifth time I couldn't help but start to giggle. That brought Jim straight up off the pull out.

"This bed really is terrible. Why on earth would you pick a pull out that's so small?"

"Gee maybe, and this is just speculation, I am short, and I don't like guests," I couldn't help but give the answer with a wicked smile.

"Ha, ha very funny."

"No really – those are the reasons. Though now I see I'm not going to get much sleep this way. Go take the bedroom and I'll take the couch. At least then you won't roll over and break an ankle."

"No, I'm not taking your bed from you. I can make up something on the floor. I'll be fine. Just go back to your room."

"I'm not going to let you sleep on the

floor. You're a guest. Take the bed."

"Ok. We both know neither of us is going to budge. So, a compromise: we share your bed but we both just sleep."

"Hmmm – I don't know. That just doesn't seem right. I mean you're still married, and you have a girlfriend. What if one or both found out?"

"If you don't tell I won't – at least this way we both can get some rest before work. Agreed?"

"Agreed. Come on. You can take the left and I'll have the right. It's a good thing I own a king size."

There was a little awkwardness at first as we both settled in. I had never shared a bed for a full night with a man. It took a little work to be comfortable with it. I was pretty sure

THE SKULL

he was struggling not to reach out and try to cuddle. He had been doing so for years with Annie and then with the new woman. Eventually I was too tired to stay awake and simply passed out.

4 HIT THE FAN

Waking up in Jim's arms was not what I had expected. I could feel his breath on the skin of my neck. I went very still and waited to see if he was awake. No change in him. Slowly I began to wiggle myself free of his embrace only to have him pull me tighter to his body. Only one way out, I sat bolt upright and swung my legs over the side of the bed. Jim rolled away but didn't seem to wake at all. I went into the bathroom and began getting ready for my day.

When I came out Jim was still asleep. Perhaps I should wake him? Or should I make breakfast first? Food first, everyone is happier when they have a full stomach. It didn't take long to get a nice breakfast made and over to the table. I kept expecting Jim to wake up with the sounds and smells, but it looked like it was going to take significantly more to get him moving. I walked back into the bedroom and put my hand on Jim's shoulder giving him a little shove as I did so.

"Hey breakfast is ready, you hungry?" I was caught completely by surprise when Jim grabbed me, hauled me down to him and rolled me back over to my side of the bed. He had again pulled me right tight against his body. This time when I tried to sit upright his arm kept me pinned to him. He began to bury his face into the top of my head. "No."

A simple word spoken with resolve. Jim's body froze in place for a moment before releasing me. At least he understood that even in his sleep addled state. I rolled off the bed and straightened my clothes before heading back into the kitchen. After a few minutes I could hear Jim moving around the bedroom followed by the shower coming on in the bathroom. I sat quietly eating my toast and bacon. Eventually Jim made his way out to the table.

"Sorry about that. I was still half asleep and thought you were Mary. It was an automatic reaction," Jim seemed truly contrite over something that really wasn't a big deal.

"It's ok, I get it. For years you've been in relationships and cuddling a person is a completely subconscious reaction. You stopped when I said no and that shows how much respect you have for the person with you. Not a lot of people would stop, in fact the few men I've dated over the years would have kept going regardless of me saying no."

"That's not right, if someone says no then there is a reason for it. You've got to respect them and what they want," Jim began to eat the scrambled eggs on his plate.

The rest of the morning went smoothly until we left for work. As we stepped outside, I could hear Annie's voice rising to a ridiculous decibel.

"You can't stop me from going up to

the door! I'm her best friend! I have a right to speak with her! You don't even have a reason for being out here!" she had gotten right in the police officer's face while she was screaming, he looked like he was considering arresting her and who could blame him?

"Annie stop, the police do have a reason for being there and you're going to end up arrested if you keep yelling at them," I had managed to get her attention with that, or perhaps it was seeing Jim standing behind me that pulled at her.

"Seriously? You had better tell me what the hell is going on here. I thought you were on my side!"

"There are no sides for me – you're my friend and Jim is my friend. I've had a bad few days and Jim came to give me a lift to work. He hadn't eaten so I offered him some breakfast while I got ready. You need to chill." The look on Annie's face could have peeled the paint off the deck.

With a little humph Annie flipped her hair and strode back to her car. She drove down the center of the road not seeming to care if there was anyone else driving there too. The cop just shook his head obviously wanting to go after her and give her a ticket yet not able to because he was supposed to stay where he was.

"Sorry Miss. She pulled up and was storming to your house. We're required to stop anyone and ask their business given the circumstances. Since she seemed a little worked up…"

"Oh, don't worry about her, she's my soon to be ex-wife. It appears she thinks Dawn should have completely cut me off even though we are friends and the three of us work together." A look of pure comprehension passed across the officer's face. He must think that Jim and I were a couple, and that Annie hadn't realized it yet.

"Well, we are off to work, are you following me around today or are you stuck watching an empty house?" I was willing to say anything to get the officer back on track.

"My partner and I are on house duty. Officer Dutch has made a full recovery. He and Andrews will be meeting you at work. If I can make a recommendation? If it's at all possible work from home as much as you can. There's less traffic on your street than downtown and we can stop anyone from coming up to the house. At work we won't know who's a possible threat."

"I'd like too but I have a few meetings and things that need to be done today. I'll try to arrange it so that I'm not in the office for most of the week."

"Dawn there is nothing at the office that is *that* urgent is there?"

"Sadly there is, I have to meet with the contractors about the new shop, Annie will insist I be present with the numbers for your presentation today, oh and there's still the matter of making sure the warehouse is up to date with the orders for the internet sales that marketing ran over the weekend. If I can get all of that done, I can work from home for the rest of the week."

"I will do everything in my power to make sure that happens," Jim seemed determined to make it all work.

The ride to the office was thankfully quiet. Andrews and Dutch met us in the parking lot. They flanked Jim and I on our way in. I decided on our way to stop and speak with Gary about the internet orders before even heading into my office. That way I could be sure to knock something off my list for today. Jim insisted on staying with me while I spoke to Gary.

"Wow, that's uh, quite the little group you've got following you around. What's going on Dawn?" Gary was casting an odd look at the three men all trying to come through his office door at the same time.

"Let's just say that my weekend didn't go as planned and leave it at that for now. How are we doing for those internet orders? Do we need to pull overtime or add extra staff to the shifts?"

"No, everything is going smoothly, since inventory was done and there were no deliveries until today, night shift had lots of time to pull orders. We're up to the minute right now. The guys are coming to pick it all up to ship in an hour or so."

"Fantastic, I'll let you get back to it then," with that I turned to see the officers and Jim playing a round of rochambeau to see who got to go through the door first. With a little smile playing at my lips, I stepped through and proceeded on to the elevator bank causing the three of them to sprint to catch up.

Andy was standing behind his desk with a handful of messages for me. One of which was the contractor saying he was running behind and if we needed, he could reschedule the meeting to tomorrow. Andy stared wide eyed at the men behind me.

"There were some issues over the weekend. The officers are going to be hanging out here for a while. Jim is going to go to his own office and get ready for his presentation. Right Jim?"

"Oh, well yeah. Of course. If you need anything just shout, ok?"

"All I need is for you to get the presentation done. Then the only thing keeping me from working at home is the contractor. Right, now I'll move everything around to get that meeting done today."

For a moment it looked like Jim wanted to reach out and give me a hug and kiss. The look passed and he walked back down the hall to his office. I could hear him barking orders at his assistant to see if everything for the drinks had been bought and was ready to go. Andrews and Dutch insisted on coming into my office and looking around before taking up their station just outside my door. The next several hours were some of the most productive of my life. No one bothered me. I was able to get all my calls done. The new furniture and display cases for the store were picked out. All my paperwork was caught up for the first time in years. A little before lunch Andy and Dutch came in.

"Here are all the numbers you need for

your lunch meeting with Annie and Jim. I know I shouldn't listen to them but are the rumors true? Are they really getting a divorce?" Andy looked concerned over the possibility.

"At this point I don't know for sure. They are seeing a counselor. I think they are trying to work things out."

"Debbie says that Jim had her call his solicitor today about getting some paperwork in order."

"Debbie shouldn't be sharing things like that. The likelihood is it's to do with getting the liquor license. The numbers for his idea look good and Jim is determined to go through with it. We may be selling specialty cocktails that are coffee and tea based once it is legal to do so."

"Ohhhh – that makes more sense than

what Debbie was saying. According to her Jim's cheating with some chick named Mary and managed to knock her up and that's why he's going to divorce Annie."

"I think I need to speak with Jim about Debbie. Was there something you needed Officer Dutch?"

"Yeah I was just letting you know that Andrews and I will be getting replaced shortly so that we can go for our lunch. We'll walk you over to the meeting and I'll stay with you while Andrews goes down and meets the others. He'll bring them up and then he and I will head off for a couple hours. Then we'll come back and have you through to the end of our shift." We walked down the hall to the conference room. I had all the paperwork and a copy of Jim's presentation. No matter what Annie thought, Jim was right about the idea. So long as we served some food as well to help absorb the alcohol we should be fine. The new location that we were renovating would be the perfect spot. There were other bars there but none served food, there weren't any actual coffee shops in the area – lots of restaurants that served coffee but not anything special. It was an up and coming area so things hadn't really taken off there yet.

Jim had everything set up. He did look a little nervous but I think that was more to do with actually making the drinks himself. There was a nice little spread of food. A good sample of the kind of thing we could serve when someone ordered. Finger sandwiches, snack foods, there were even a few deserts cakes that could be eaten with fingers and leave little to no mess. I was impressed. Annie was the last to arrive and she had a look of someone who had already decided that this was over. That it wasn't happening or if it was it would be over her dead body.

Behind her came Debbie, Andy, and Charmaine. I had made sure Andy would be there to take minutes. Jim had probably enlisted Debbie to help serve the drinks. There was no reason for Annie's assistant Charmaine to be there though. In fact, I don't recall having even seen her for the last few weeks. It was rare that Annie needed her since she always just came straight to me with anything that she felt was beneath her notice.

"I mean really do we need to have the cops standing right outside the door? It looks terrible to people. Like we're going to be arrested or something. We don't even need to have this meeting; we aren't selling those drinks in my shops and that's that."

"Annie, you promised to listen to the numbers. Part of that is presenting it and showing you what could be done. You also promised that if the numbers were good that Jim could do what he wanted."

"I said no such thing," she tilted her chin up and clenched her jaw. It was obvious that she wasn't going to give in without a fight. She plunked herself into a chair and proceeded to turn herself away from everything.

Jim began the presentation. Everything was going smoothly until a commotion outside interrupted everything. A rather petite woman who was obviously pregnant was outside the door trying to get through, but the officers weren't allowing it. She was visibly upset.

"Mary?" The confusion on Jim's face swept over to concern. He bolted out of the office and into the hall. So, this was his new lady. She was weeping and breathing heavily. One of the officers grabbed his radio and said something. The other was pulling a chair over from the open area by Annie's office and helping her sit.

"Who the fuck is that?" Annie's voice had gone so hard and cold it sent chills down my spine.

"That is Mary. She and Jim met a while back. Something about her leaving her abusive husband. I think Jim let her stay at the spare apartment for a while until she found herself a place that was safe." A heavily edited version of what I knew and leaving out the fact that she was now living in Annie's house having Jim's baby.

"What apartment?"

"The one Jim kept so that when the two of you had an argument, he could go get drunk and crash somewhere safe that didn't need him to drive. He got rid of it a few weeks ago because he quit drinking about six months ago and has been sober ever since."

"You knew about this?"

"Only very recently. Jim admitted it right around the time that you moved out." The look on Annie's face spoke of pure betrayal. The problem is that she had been lying to Jim for just as long about her own affair and she still hadn't admitted to it. Though she had also lied to me about that as well. I turned away from Annie so that I didn't have to see that she wanted to pounce on me. The assistants had all made their way over to the window wall and were leaning back against the table watching as some paramedics put Mary on to a stretcher and leave. Jim looked deeply conflicted about what to do. He turned and came back into the conference room.

"I need to speak with you and Dawn alone ok Annie?" He glanced at the little group who immediately began to file out. They didn't go far though and grouped up a little way down the hall to watch.

"Well, we're alone now – what do you have to say for yourself?"

"Look I made a mistake. I'm sure you are probably questioning if the baby is mine. I thought it was. Mary just admitted that she has been seeing her husband almost since the day we met and that she is pretty sure the baby is his. I'm going to request a DNA test once the baby is born. Just to confirm. She was getting her stuff together to move back in with her husband when she said something felt wrong. Mary didn't want to go to the hospital but if there is something wrong with her or the baby that's where she needs to be. I'm going to head there." With heavy eyes Jim turned and went back out the door.

"How much of this did you know?"

"Some not all. I was sworn to secrecy. He was planning to tell you at the first counselling session. You know, the one that you didn't show up for. Then told me that he had been so drunk he probably forgot that he'd been there. You can't be mad at me when you're just as guilty as he is for cheating."

"I can't do this today. I'm going back to my apartment. You can handle everything that comes in. If you still want to work here when I take Jim for every dime he has I suggest you learn where your loyalty really lies." With that said she grabbed her purse, stormed from the room and headed down the hall to the elevator.

I gestured to the little threesome to come back into the conference room. After sharing a few looks they came and settled into their seats.

"What you've seen and heard goes no further than us. It could destroy the company and cost us all our jobs if anyone outside of here found out. Right now I need all of you to help me out. I don't think Annie is going to come back for the next week and with Jim thoroughly distracted by the Mary situation I'm the one who is going to be handling everything. Okay, any meetings that the two of them had planned should be rescheduled. Take messages for all calls and bring them to Andy to sort. I'll do my best to keep things running. Agreed?"

Lots of nodding later I sent the three of them off to deal with their duties. I sat for a moment thinking about what I could do next. With a sigh I realized that I needed to clean up the mess in the conference room so that I could use it for a meeting with the contractor. I packed up all the food and took it down to my office. At least I'd get a meal at some point.

The meeting with the contractor went off without a hitch. I made several changes to suit what Jim would need for his coffee bar idea. Annie was going to throw a fit, but she left it to me and the numbers worked. I was starving as I went back to my office – Dutch and Andrews were back in their positions. I settled at my desk with some of the snacks from earlier. As I worked through everything, I ate. It was the chocolate cake that tasted a little funny. Normally I love anything chocolate, but this tasted almost metallic. I only had one bite before I tossed it into the waste bin. After a minute or two I began to feel sick and woozy. I got up and headed for my office door, but my throat felt like it

THE SKULL

was swelling and cutting off my
breathing. Everything went dark.

5 HOME

When I woke up the same doctor was looking down at me. He seemed more concerned and less judgmental this time. Probably because the police were also standing there.

"That was a close one. It seems someone poisoned you. "We're waiting to see what the mixture was but at this time you're going to be ok," the doctor seemed pleased with his statement.

As much as I wanted to be happy all I felt was pain. My entire abdomen felt like it was on fire. A cramp hit and caused me to curl around myself in an attempt to ease the pain. I tried to speak to the doctor, but I couldn't seem to catch my breath.

"Yes, that will happen every once in a while. We are doing what we can to treat your symptoms while we wait for the blood work to come back. Then we can be more specific about what we will do," the doctor turned and went to speak with Andrews while Dutch stood by and kept one eye on me.

It felt like hours before the doctor received the information even though it could only have been a few minutes. He promptly started ordering the nurses around and an IV was inserted into my hand. He took a syringe and shot something into the IV tube. Slowly the cramping eased, and the pain stopped. I was able to breathe and speak without as much pain. Andrews and Dutch stayed with me each step of the way. When it became clear that I was going to be held overnight they spoke with the doctor and got me a private room which made their job easier. Once I had been settled Dutch came in to speak with me.

"I went back to the office and had your assistant pack up what you'll need. I have to ask you a few questions. It's obvious that someone has tried to get to you again. Can you take me through what you were doing and what happened?"

After hearing what I had to say he made a call to the on-scene group and made sure they had collected my garbage. They would test the cake and see. To me that had to be the source. The question now was who had put the poison in the cake? It could have been done at any time before or during the meeting. Whoever was trying to kill me didn't seem to care if they caught anyone else accidentally. After all who could be sure that I'd be the one or the only one eating that piece of cake?

It was all too exhausting to think about. I called Lynn and told her to stay home. I had been informed that my emergency contact had been notified. She wasn't happy about it to say the least, but she had other things to worry about at the moment. Talking with her was a nice distraction from the mess that was my life.

"I don't know what's gotten into Mark lately. It seems like any time I want to spend some time together – even to watch a show he likes – he just has more work. He's never had this much before and I'm a little worried."

"Don't worry about him. He probably has taken on the extra so that when he gets his paternity leave you guys won't be too short. After all, he only gets what? 75% of his wage? He's probably just socking away the extra so there's no dip in income."

"You're right. But then, you usually are. I'll try to be more understanding. I am just getting so bored! With you not available and Mark always gone I've been hanging with Mom a lot more. I still haven't told her about the baby since I'm not showing yet and she's been asking why I'm spending all my time with her. I promise I haven't told her what's happening with you but she's getting suspicious. You may need to get a boyfriend as an excuse," there was a thread of laughter in her voice. After all I hadn't dated in years.

"Ha ha very funny. You can tell her all the gossip I've got from work. It may take a while to tell you everything but then you'll have lots of fuel to keep mom at bay."

The next hour was spent explaining what was going on with Annie and Jim, with the new changes happening, the new store and orders. By the end Lynn was starting to fall asleep but was thrilled with all the information. I'd assured her I was fine and that once I was able to be around her without being a threat to her life I'd spend as much time as I could with her.

THE SKULL

* * * * *

I woke up the next morning and Andrews was sitting in the chair next to my bed. He was bent over with his craggy old face in both hands. After a moment it was like he sensed me staring at him. He pulled his hands away from his face and sat up straighter in the chair.

"Welcome back."

"I wasn't aware that I was gone," that kind of statement didn't bode well for me.

"You've been giving the doctors a run for their money. I don't know what they gave you the first time but you seemed ok. Then you coded. Three times. We weren't sure you would make it after the last one. I have to hand it to you, you're quite a fighter.

You just refused to give up. Just so you know it's been a week since you were poisoned." Andrews looked like he'd aged a couple decades during our conversation.

"Who knows?" If they had called my sister again she'd be in rough shape. I doubt they'd have let her come and sit with me given the circumstances.

"No one. Just those of us in charge of you and our boss. He wants to use you to draw out the killer. The problem is that there's rumors now. Some think that you're dead. Others think you're alive. For your sake I can only hope that the person that's after you thinks he finished the job." Andrews heaved a huge sigh of exhaustion.

"I don't know what I want more – the guy trying to kill me laying off or coming after me again so he can be caught. Skull is still on me, no changes there."

"We'll take you home in another day or so. The doctor wants to be sure all the poison is out of your system."

"Can I get my computer? I need to see what is happening at the company. I need to speak with Jim and Annie. Did they ever confirm where the poison came from?"

"Yeah – piece of chocolate cake. Thing is that it wasn't the only thing that was poisoned. You had a glass on your desk with some kind of alcohol in it. It showed a different kind of poison than what was in the cake. That's what the doctor said. They had treated you for the first kind of poison but weren't aware of the second until it was nearly too late. We've checked everything else and you should be fine now. As for your computer: you can have it and look at the messages but you aren't allowed to answer them yet. Same with your phone. I'll get Dutch to bring them in while I call my boss and let him know you're conscious."

Andrews slowly stood – I could hear his joints popping as he did. He left closing the door quietly. I searched around and found the controls to adjust the bed. As I slowly sat up it felt like my abdomen had been beaten on with a bat. I was sore everywhere. A bone deep ache. I couldn't help but wonder when I'd be allowed out of this place. Dutch walked in with a bag in his hands. Inside were my purse, laptop, cellphone and charger. Quietly Dutch helped me plug everything in.

"Once I knew you were going to be here for a while I went out and got an extension cord for you. After all we don't want to pull the plug on you just so you can charge your phone." A sly grin slid across Dutch's face. I couldn't help smiling back even if I didn't feel up to laughing yet. Some of my favorite memes are the ones where a kid unplugs the parents' life support to charge their phone. Looks like Dutch finds them funny too.

"I love those memes. I send them to my mother every time she complains that I love my phone more than her."

"Same here, though it's my father that is the tech phobic one in my family." Dutch's voice had a slight huskiness to it. Almost like he'd been crying for an extended length of time.

"Are you ok?"

"I'm alright. I'm still getting the odd headache after that hit to the head. Doctors are saying that it'll pass." Dutch proceeded to take the chair Andrews had vacated. He repositioned it so that he could read emails and text messages over my shoulder.

There were lots. Most of the emails came from the assistants asking if I was ok and wondering who they should speak with to keep the company going. Andy had sent an email letting me know that he was doing his best to make decisions and hold down the fort for me until I was able to take over again. He also let me know that he was in direct contact with Jim but that he hadn't been able to get a hold of Annie.

The text messages were far worse. Jim at first letting me know that Mary was ok for the moment. She'd been given bed rest to help get the baby settled and to take the stress off of her. Then slowly over the course of the day his messages got more worried as I didn't answer him. Eventually there was one that said Andy had messaged and told him what had happened at work. He asked that as soon as I was well enough to message and let him know I was ok. If he hadn't heard from me in a couple days he was going to come down to the hospital and sit with me. Interspersed with these were messages from my sister and mother. At first, they were pleasant just touching base type messages. Lynn's slowly became more and more frantic as I didn't answer followed with a message that stated she'd been called by a doctor who had informed her of what had happened and that she wasn't allowed to visit at this time. After that every day she would send a long message letting me know what had happened in her day and how the little whale was doing. Mom's messages simply grew in worry until she started using the phrase "young lady" when demanding I call her. Shortly after the first of those messages came one apologizing and saying that Lynn had told her all about the issues at work with Annie and Jim. That she understood I was basically running the company on my own at the moment and that if I wanted, she could run fresh groceries to my house for me.

The messages from Annie were the worst of the lot. All she spoke of was her new man and how I was a terrible friend for choosing Jim over her. That she didn't want to speak to me ever again and that if there was any work business that needed to be handled to have Andy send the messages. There were a couple messages from her lawyer as well. These were mostly showing me that I didn't have a dominant share in the business and a cash offer to buy me out with a note that once the buyout was completed I would be free to pursue other avenues for a career.

"I wouldn't take that offer if I was you." Dutch sat shaking his head.

"Wasn't planning on it. I'm the one who's been running the business for years. I know what all the numbers are. With the changes we just made – I guess it was a week ago now – the company will be worth more than triple what it was. Even with just 25% of the shares I could wait to sell and make ten times more than that offer. She just wants me gone since I know about her affair, and I backed Jim on the innovations." I closed my laptop with a sigh. After shifting things around a bit I was able to rest comfortably. Andrews walked in just as I was beginning to doze off again.

"I spoke with my boss and we are going to let you go home as soon as you are cleared by the doctor. We've been looking into your contacts and think you are safe enough to speak with James Barkley and Lynn Weatherstone. Other than that, no contact with anyone else until they've been fully vetted." Andrews looked relieved by what he was saying.

"I guess I'm not dead yet eh?"

"Not yet," Andrews cracked a smile over the comment. Dutch looked so shocked he would have fallen over if he hadn't been sitting in the chair.

When I was finally released it was cold and gloomy out. Rain was pelting the police car as we pulled into my driveway. There were police still sitting on the deck outside. I was ok with that. My car was sitting in the driveway. I thought about starting it to make sure it still ran. It had been cold the last couple nights and I hadn't used it in days. Andrews glanced in the rearview mirror as if checking to see if I was still there. It's odd how things worked out. He had been the biggest skeptic when he'd seen the skull the first time we'd met. Now it was like he was determined to help me survive regardless of the tattoo. As we walked up the porch I could see lights on inside my house.

"Welcome home!" Jim was standing there with Lynn. A huge meal was laid out on my counters.

"Mom tried to bring fresh groceries, but she didn't have the key anymore. When I tried mine, it didn't work either. Thankfully Jim pulled up and let me in." Lynn swooped me up into a hug.

"That's right – I got the locks changed after my stuff was left at the park. I didn't want any unexpected visitors. I have a key set aside for you but I just haven't had a chance to give it to you. Also, the code for the security system." It felt as if the air was being pushed out of my lungs.

"Don't worry – I know that she's your

back up so I went ahead and gave her both once we got in here." Jim was leaning against the counter looking exhausted. "Let's have a nice dinner and then I have a few things to go over with you from work and with what's happening with Annie."

"That sounds good. I have some emails and texts I think you should look at Jim," After a few struggles I was finally able to push my sister's arms off of me.

Dinner turned out to be a make your own wrap event. Lynn wasn't big on cooking – she preferred to bake so Jim had made up all the separate items and for the first time ever my wrap warmer was used. I had bought it years ago with the intention of making my own fajita wraps but had never gotten around to pulling it out.

Lynn ate and caught me up on what was happening with our parents. She had managed to lie to them convincingly enough that they thought I was travelling around to the different stores to keep things running that way. Silly since they knew I could do all those things with a phone call from the comfort of my office.

"Thank you for keeping them in the dark for the moment. I don't know what they would do if they knew the truth."

"It's not going to get you much further. They're going to find out eventually. Don't waste time trying to evade a killer if you aren't spending time with your family before it's all over." Lynn was ever the optimist. With a quick hug she was heading home again. I could feel Jim step up behind me and look out as an officer helped Lynn into her car. Even though the main streets had cleared up there was still lots of ice patches on my little back street.

"I'm not letting you die you know." The softly spoken statement from Jim wasn't unexpected. We'd had conversations about the tattoos over the years.

"I know. I'm not letting me die either." The small reassurance seemed to cause Jim to relax and let out a breath he'd been holding in. "What's the news?"

"Andy has been a huge help in keeping things running at the office. I had to let go of both Charmaine and Debbie. The two of them were spreading rumors and I found out they were working together to try and sabotage my standing in the company. Apparently, Annie made them the offer to take over both of our positions if they helped her get rid of us. I spoke with my lawyer and he's working on the divorce. If all goes to plan then Annie will still hold shares and have voting rights but she won't be involved in the day to day running of the company. As for Mary, she's still having issues. I took her back to the hospital and her husband showed up. It got bad. They called security to have him removed. They're keeping her under observation and pumping her full of fluids. The latest scans haven't been able to find the baby's heartbeat. They aren't saying it out loud yet, but I think this isn't going to work out." The sadness in Jim's face was painful to see. He had always wanted to be a father.

"I'm sorry Jim. I wish there was something I could do about it. Here, all I've got are these ridiculous threats Annie sent." I showed him the phone messages and the emails from her lawyer. As he read through his face went from bright red to deathly white.

"Did she really think you'd accept this?"

"I'm not sure she's in her right mind anymore. If you need any evidence about the affair or her irrational behavior, you can show your lawyer copies of these. Tell him I had been poisoned and was in the hospital at the time they were received. That should get you some sympathy in court."

"Thanks Dawn," a small half smile crossed Jim's face. "Alright. I'll help clean up and then we will have

THE SKULL

popcorn and a movie. Then I'll head home. No work for you, though I will probably send you some bits to check. Andy is very helpful but there are a few things that need your special touch."

6 STALLED

Then there was nothing. For months. No attempts on my life. No break-ins. Just day after day of work. Mary had gone back to her husband and ended up losing the baby. Annie continued to live in her apartment and see her married boyfriend with more and more frequency. She stopped coming in to work only showing up about once a month. Jim ended up going back to his house but he would come and spend every weekend with me. He'd gotten the divorce papers drawn up and had given them to Annie who promptly lost them. She did this several times until Jim finally had the lawyer send someone with them, they still weren't signed.

Lynn was getting closer and closer to her due date. She'd stopped hanging out with mom once she hit the stage where she was visibly pregnant. I couldn't believe she was keeping this a secret. What was odder was that mom still hadn't had the tattoo appear for her grandchild yet. Lynn thought it was because she hadn't shared the news yet. I didn't believe that. There had to be another reason. Even the police had pulled their officers off of watching the house. I was very glad for that security system Jim had installed, I was still jumpy. I still had a

THE SKULL

skull. I'd never heard of someone lasting a year with one. I had stopped trying to keep it hidden since it seemed like everyone except my parents knew. When I had to visit with them I made sure to cover it up. Summer had struck with a reckless abandonment. I was tired of hiding in my home when the weather was so beautiful. Inevitably I let my guard down when I shouldn't have.

I was out in my backyard. It wasn't big but I had made it over so that there were little sitting areas on one side and large veg patch on the other. At the back I had put in trees that had only reached their maturity a year or so ago. They looked like I'd have a large crop of fruits and nuts this year. I was weeding the veg patch when I felt like I was being watched. The hair had begun to stand up on the back of my neck. I took a steadying breath and slowly began to rise. I was pretending I was going to grab the hose so I could water everything. As I approached the hose next to the steps, I bolted into my house and locked the door behind me.

I ducked down in the hopes that if the person was going to shoot me, they'd aim higher and miss. I worked my way along the floor at a crawl towards the front. I could see the door there was locked. I turned and cut towards my bedroom. The wall with the French doors was on the inside. I could use that and the closet as a way to block shots from being taken at me. I pulled my cell phone out of my pocket and waited. All I could hear was the beating of my own heart and my harsh breathing.

Slowly sounds from outside began to filter in. There was a banging happening at the back door. I dialed 911. After a short time, I could hear the sirens approaching. The noise at the back door stopped. Once the police arrived, I told them what had happened. There were footprints on the back porch and it looked like whoever it was had tried to break the door down.

"It's a good thing you have a thick door and stout locks. He'd have had that door down otherwise. The forensic people will be here to gather what they can. Then the house is yours again. I'd suggest having someone come and stay with you or going to someone else's house for the night. Just as a precaution."

That said I called Jim to let him know

what had happened. He came over with a bag to spend the night. We'd gotten comfortable sharing a bed over the last few months.

"I can't say that I'm surprised. After all they never caught the guy that tried to kill you and now that the police presence is gone it was only a matter of time," Jim settled into his spot on the couch.

"I know – I just hoped that the guy had moved on or gotten caught elsewhere and that I wasn't still his target. After all it has been a long time," I snuggled down next to him.

"At least you were still on guard enough to notice that something was wrong, get inside safe and call the cops. You really do have great senses." When he looked down at me, I realized

I was still in little more than a low-cut tank top and the short shorts that I wore when working in the garden. He had to be getting a great view from above me.

"I'm going to go shower and then we can discuss dinner." With a little hop off the couch, I whipped around the far end and was off to my room. I caught a glimpse of Jim following me with his eyes as I walked away.

A shower and some light but covering clothing later I came out of my room to find Jim sprawled out in front of the TV, asleep. It had gotten late. The light outside was just beginning to fade. I walked around and made sure that the doors were locked, and the alarm was set. Then I started working on dinner. I'd brought in some of the fresh veg that had ripened before I'd started weeding this morning. With some grilled chicken I could make a nice salad. The fruit could all be cut up and added to a bowl with some sugar syrup in it – with some whipped cream it would be a nice dessert.

Jim woke just as I was cutting up the fruit. In complete silence he came over and started helping. I couldn't help but feel tense. There seemed to be no rhyme or reason for me being targeted again. I could only hope that I survived. After a quiet dinner we put the dishes in the dishwasher and Jim headed to the bathroom. I sat watching TV not really paying any attention to what was on.

"Is that Annie?" The incredulousness in Jim's voice caused me to jump and focus on the TV.

"I think it is," there was some reality show on that was talking about celebrity break ups and where they were now. Annie appeared to be at a bar in the clip they were showing. She stood up from a table of other women that all looked a lot like her and as she did, so she managed to flash everyone.

I looked over at Jim. He was beet red and had closed his eyes. I knew what he was thinking. Here was one of the CEOs of our company flashing a camera. This was going to cause all kinds of issues. We needed to call the lawyers and get ahead of this.

The calls took all night, but we had a statement being released, an apology as well and they were going to speak to Annie about being less visible for a while. If all went well, we wouldn't have too big a dip in the profits.

Neither of us got much sleep that night.

We both were awake at a ridiculous hour the next morning and decided we needed to head to work early. When we arrived at the office there were cameras and people wanting comments waiting at the edge of the lot. We went up and found all the lawyers had taken over the conference room. They were sitting across from Annie who was dressed as though she'd just come from the bar. She looked like she may still be drunk, and she was openly shouting back at the lawyers.

Jim followed me into my office. We both stood with our backs leaning against the door. Completely silent other than the muffled sound of Annie shouting.

"Do you think she even understands what she's done to the company?" Jim seemed numb, his voice completely devoid of emotion.

"Honesty right now I think she's so drunk she doesn't understand why they aren't serving her another drink, let alone that she's not at a bar anymore. Did she always drink like this? I mean I knew you drank but I never saw her."

"Oh yeah, she'd say hey let's have a couple drinks and before you know it, we were both completely hammered. It went like that for years. I tried quitting and getting help so many times, but she would always come purring up to me on nights when I'd been sober for a while and whisper in my ear about how one wouldn't hurt. I'd always give in. It's my fault too." It was the most mature thing I'd ever heard Jim say.

"For now, let's just focus on getting work done. The opening for the new shop is soon and I don't want to miss any of the little details."

Jim left me to my work and went off to do his. Eventually Annie's yelling stopped, and the knock came at my door for us to go see what the lawyers had to say about the current situation. It wasn't good but having caught it last night it also wasn't as bad as it could have been.

7 LEMONS

When life gives you lemons you should make lemonade. A wonderful line. Except if we examine it closely you will discover that lemons are not naturally occurring, they were created. A long time ago – say sometime before 700 AD – someone decided to cross breed a bitter orange and a citron. Boom! Lemons. That's right. Life didn't give us lemons. We created them for ourselves.

Why this little exploration into the life

of a lemon you ask? Mostly because I kept getting them flung at me. With Annie's bad behavior Jim cut off all the access she had to our corporate accounts and their personal ones. This caused Annie to move back into the house where Jim was living. Creating a massive fight over who got what in the divorce. This led to Jim needing a place to stay. Guess who he decided to move in with? Yup.

Meanwhile I was nearly hit by a car when I went to meet Lynn for lunch. Then she confided in me that she thought Mark was having an affair – she had discovered some undergarments in one of the guest rooms that were definitely not hers. Oh, and out of the blue there's mom and dad walking over towards us. I looked down at my uncovered arm and it was like that damn skull was laughing up at me. There's nothing I could do.

"There's our girls! Lynn! Is this why you've been avoiding spending time with me?"

"No, well yeah kinda. Ok yes, I am pregnant. It's a little whale. I just didn't want to tell you until I was certain that everything in my life was going ok. I think Mark is cheating on me."

"No matter what, don't move out! Kick him out first. That way you're more likely to get the house in the divorce."

"Wow mom! That's downright mercenary! Any other tips? I could pass some of them on to Jim," I should never have chimed in. It just drew her attention to me. She stared at me for a moment before a look of horror crossed her face. My mother had seen the skull.

"Oh, my honey! How long has that been there?" She was on the verge of weeping openly – something that was strictly forbidden during her upbringing. My father pressed her down into the empty chair and then settled down in the other.

"A few months. It's nothing to be worried about. I have this entirely under control."

"Entirely under control. A few months. Are you insane? You kept this from us – we may not have much time left with you! We all know what that skull means!" Her words were soft and controlled at first but by the end she was red with anger and barely keeping her voice down.

"Yes, mother I know. Let's get you and father something to eat and I will explain everything."

After the first hour I called Jim to let him know that my parents had found out about the skull and that I was stuck at the restaurant until I had caught them up on everything. Then I finished the rest. I couldn't believe how much had happened in such a short time.

"Well, where is this police protection then?" My father was looking around expecting to see cops at every table.

"They pulled it a while ago. There were no more attempts on my life, and they think he gave up."

"There must be a reason for the skull.

It doesn't just appear without reason. No one has survived more than 5 months. How long has it been on you?"

"It showed up around mid-February, so I'm heading into my 6th month." The look of astonishment on my family's faces spoke volumes. Funnily enough it gave me hope that I would survive this. That's when it struck me that it had already been half a year since I had this tattoo. I'd set a world record.

"We need to throw Lynn her baby shower soon then. When are you due honey?"

"Around the end of September to the beginning of October according to the doctor. It's a boy." Lynn was happy to talk about the baby and the shower. I quietly said my goodbye and went back to the office. Jim was waiting to pounce on me when I came out of the elevator.

"How'd they take it?" Genuine concern in his voice.

"Not well but not as badly as I thought but that could be due to being in public. They were astonished at how long Lynn had hidden the baby from them and equally shocked at how long I'd had my skull."

"Maybe we should call it a day and head home early. I think we both need a break."

There was little to do other than gather our things and let our assistant know that we were leaving for the day. The drive home was peaceful. Right up until the semi crushed the side of the car.

I awoke in a hospital bed. I didn't feel like I was in bad shape. In the bed next to me was Jim. He was looking a little worse for the wear. The truck hit us on the driver's side, but Jim had been speeding up to get through the intersection. We'd gotten lucky. The focal point had been the back half of the car. I could hear weeping coming from near Jim's bed. Annie was sitting there looking flawless with big tears rolling down her cheeks as she stared up at the policeman and doctor that were standing there.

From what I was hearing she was playing the part of the grief-stricken, soon to be ex-wife who still had feelings for her husband but also felt mixed emotions because he was living with her best friend, and we all knew what that could mean. It was all so tawdry. I didn't like it one bit. After everything that had happened. I couldn't let it stand.

"Oh please. You're just sad that you're having to be here. Let me guess you're still listed as his emergency contact? He really should get that fixed." Annie went from flawless crying to ugly red and furious in seconds.

"I had to leave a group of friends at the bar for this! Yeah, I am sad, after all you chose him over me! I'm your best friend and you chose him!" The glint in her eyes was enough for me to know she was feeling triumphant about her performance. All the noise was causing Jim to wake up. He took one look at Annie and gestured the doctor over. After a quiet conversation the doctor led Annie from the room.

"Sorry about that. I forgot to change her as my contact. Why do I hurt everywhere?"

"Cause we got hit by a truck." The pain meds were making me feel a little loopy. The policeman looked at the two of us.

"Look folks I hate to be the bearer of bad news but that was no accident. The truck had been sitting at that light three or four times before it suddenly rammed you. We couldn't find the driver. After crashing he jumped out and disappeared into the crowd."

I let the information settle in my mind. Things were escalating again. I needed to figure it out. But I was just so sore and tired.

* * * * *

After a couple days we were both discharged. At home Jim and I cleaned up and he ordered a new car. We'd just have to use mine for the time being. Something had been stewing in the back of my mind while we had been stuck in bed. With a glance at Jim, I knew now was the time to brooch the topic.

"We need to set a trap. If we do, then this whole thing would be over. I'd have to be bait. You could hire anyone you wanted to help with protection."

"No. It's too big a risk. I'm not going to lose you. I don't think I could live with that."

"At this rate not only will I get killed but with you spending most of your time with me you could get caught in the crossfire – look what happened today! I can't live even for a short time with that on my hands. Please consider this. We could involve the police. I still have Dutch's number."

"He's probably disappointed you didn't call him sooner," Jim was chuckling over the memory of Dutch hitting on me after explaining that they were pulling the officers off protection detail.

"I'm doing this whether you like it or not. You can have a hand in it, or you can stay out of my way."

"Ok, we will figure this out together then. First, we need to come up with a plan, then we can call in anyone we want to fill in positions to keep you safe. Do you have any idea at all who is after you?"

"There can only be three people. I

have no idea which one it is. Heck it could be all of them."

"Alright, let's sit down and get started."

We stayed up all night working on our plans. Fleshing out every single detail. Morning came and went with phone calls. Making every arrangement that we could.

When we woke the air conditioner had kicked on and was running full bore. The timing was terrible. The end of summer had gotten so hot that no one was doing anything. There was a full stop to all our plans as we closed most of the shops during the daytime hours since the air conditioning wasn't doing enough to make things cool. They were calling it a heat dome. Even at night it didn't get cool. Jim and I called everyone to let them know we were going to wait for this heat to pass before trying to draw out my killer. I've never been good with patience. All my plants died, and my trees were struggling. I did everything I could.

Work was only happening at night. During the day Jim and I stayed home and did nothing. It left me with a lot of time to think. To plan. I still had to get Lynn's baby shower figured out. Even with a skull tattoo my mother wasn't going to let me not attend. Then I was suddenly the host for the whole event. I could only hope that the heat didn't kill me first.

"Why didn't I let that guy kill me before this happened? Why did I have to be so stubborn?" I was lying on the floor in the living room with the a/c unit pumping as much cold out as it could while a fan took the cool air and ran it across my body. Every so often I would turn over or move to one side as the floor got warm underneath me.

"Don't even joke about that. We're lucky, we have air conditioning. There's lots of people out there trying to find places to stay cool." Jim had probably had enough of my complaints at this point. I didn't care. I didn't know that my scalp could sweat the way it was.

I had managed to order all the supplies for the baby shower online. Every time the doorbell rang Jim would have the delivery person stand inside for a few minutes to let them cool down. I stocked bottles of water and kept them cold as best I could, giving them out to anyone and everyone who came past. A fire broke out in the neighborhood just a few houses down from mine. The fire department didn't want us to leave right away but to be prepared in case there was a change in the direction of the fire or if a spark lit several others.

It was a long night that night. We could see the red light of the fire as the houses burned to the ground. The smell was awful. It felt like my throat was clogged from the smoke. At one point Jim covered his face with a wet bandana and went out to the side of the house to clear the mess off the air conditioning. He was concerned that the debris from the air would clog it and cause it to die on us. That would have been lethal in the heat wave.

Watching the news, we found out it had been arson. A man had been seen tossing a bottle into the house that had started burning first. Shivers had run down my back when I heard that. The only thing that had saved most of the houses on the street was that there was no wind at all for the days that everything was burning. We saw reports of towns completely wiped out because of a single spark catching and the wind pushing the fire through the towns. Then setting other fires as ember rode the wind to tinder dry buildings and grasses. Jim insisted that all the employees retain full pay and then created an emergency fund as a precaution against any home losses. I made the suggestion that we offer to purchase air conditioners for all of them as well. Word got around the stores and the offices. There were only a couple of people who didn't contact us for one.

One night when we were just getting home from work at sunrise Jim noticed a package sitting on the deck. Unusual since it was only a few businesses like ours that were allowing nighttime work hours. It looked like it was leaking. I'm not sure what was in it, but it was defiantly dead. Jim called the cops and they made sure it was safe for us to be in the house. We gave them a copy of the camera footage. Dutch called to let us know that the box had been dropped by a large guy in a hoodie. Jim decided that we needed more cameras and this time facing the street. A few hours later everything was set up and the security men were off to find a cool place to stay.

Lynn began coming over and hanging out with me every day towards the end of August. She couldn't seem to get comfortable and things between her and Mark were at an all-time low.

"I'm sure that he's cheating I found a second phone in his office that he had locked up in the drawer of his desk. He changed the password for the security camera software so that I can't access the account. I don't even know how far back he did it since I trusted him with everything. Do you guys know anyone that may have the ability to crack in to his stuff for me?" Lynn kept shifting around in her seat and rubbing a spot on her belly where the baby was kicking her.

"I can see but our firm employs his for all our IT stuff. That's one of the reasons he got to where he is in the company. Bet he didn't tell you that he was on the verge of being fired when he came to me and asked if we would move to them for our IT needs. After landing the account he got promoted." I shook my head over the situation. I remembered it very clearly. Our corporate contract had come due and the support we'd been getting had been dismal. I was in the market and knowing that my sister would have been in a bad spot if Mark had lost his job was enough for me to throw the contracts his way.

"I remember that vaguely – I think I was drinking at the office at that point. Annie was totally against it. You campaigned hard for us to go to such a small local group. She and I got in a fight, and I ended up voting your way." Jim was standing in front of the island in the kitchen making us some lunch while Lynn and I chatted at the dining table.

"I had no idea. Seems he's been hiding things from me since the beginning. I know that he told me you had changed to his company for IT support, we had just gotten married I was still working as a TA at the university to help make ends meet at the time. We still had that crumby little shoe box apartment downtown."

"Your baby shower is only a few weeks away and not long after that you are due. So, here's my question to you: what are you going to do? You started to suspect the affair a while ago. You've been trying to find evidence other than that bra. What are you going to do once you have the evidence?"

"I'm not sure. Divorce seems the most likely scenario but I want what's best for my baby – I'd really like Mark to be in the picture so I guess counselling first? Maybe we can sort it out." Lynn didn't seem to be so sure about the direction she should take.

"I'd like to chime in here – counselling regardless of if your spouse shows up or not is worth your time. If you do end up divorced then having someone to speak with that isn't a friend or family member is helpful. I managed to get to the root of a number of my problems. I kept going to my counselor even though Annie never showed to any of the appointments." It was true, Jim had stabilized mentally and emotionally after he and Annie had split. Every now and then he would take an hour or two and go for an appointment.

"Thank you, Jim. I'm going to speak

with Mark about it soon. After the guy comes to fix the air conditioning. It died a couple weeks ago; I've basically been staying on the ground floor with fans on me. He said that they were coming last week but no one showed up and there was a funny chemical smell in and around the house. There's been no one at the door – the app would have pinged my phone."

"Where has Mark been this whole time? You can come and stay here with us. Jim and I can take the couch and you can have the bedroom." I had a bad feeling about what Lynn had said.

"Oh, he's been staying at work most of the time. At least that's what he told me. I think his mistress has a/c and so he's staying with her as much as he can. I swung past his office one evening when he said he was working late and he wasn't there. No – I can't boot you out of your room. I'm ok at home really."

"No. You're coming and staying here. I'll look into a different company for you so that you can get the house cool again. Dawn, why don't you and Lynn go and pack some things for her after dinner? That way it's cool enough to be in the house. Since you and I are working at night anyways it won't be a big deal for Lynn to have the bedroom. They are saying that the heat dome will end in a couple weeks but that it will still be hot for a couple more after that." Jim sat our lunches in front of us and promptly dug in to his.

Lynn couldn't argue with him. I made her take a nap in the bedroom while Jim and I crashed on the pull out for the rest of the afternoon. As soon as sun set Lynn and I took my car the four blocks to her place. Heat poured out when she opened the door. We stood for a couple minutes out front hoping it would cool down a bit. When we went in it was stifling. Lynn went upstairs and opened the windows to vent the house a little more while she packed her things. I did the same on the ground floor. I could smell something was off in the kitchen. Probably the garbage had heated up and was causing a stink. With Lynn so far along I didn't want her trying to take it out on her own so I went ahead and opened the cabinet.

I gagged at the scent. It wasn't garbage. There in the cabinet with her mixer was a decapitated rat. No traps were in site. For a moment I stood there unsure how to proceed. The sound of Lynn moving up on the second floor brought me to my senses. I opened the cabinet under the sink so I could get the garbage can. There was another rat there too. After scooping them up I began to check each cupboard and sure enough there were headless rats in every single one. I wandered around room to room after that just to be sure there were none hidden anywhere else. Stepping outside with the garbage bag I couldn't help but wonder if this was supposed to be a warning to Lynn from the mistress. The problem was no one knew that Lynn suspected Mark of an affair other than Jim, mom, dad and I. Walking back into the house the smell had significantly reduced. Lynn was sitting at the island waiting for me.

"What were you doing?"

"Oh the garbage down here was stinking the place up so I took it out for you. Better than coming back to a house that reeks right?" Until I was sure what was going on I didn't want to tell Lynn about all the decapitated rats.

"You're so sweet. Come on – let's hit the grocery store before we go back to your place. I want ice cream and pickles. Maybe some peanut butter too. I heard that the nursery is open late now. We could get you some new plants for when the weather cools."

We came home with far too many weird food items and a car full of plants that would never survive in my yard. It didn't matter, I was just happy that my sister wasn't going be sick or alone in that house. If she had been alone. How did all those rats get there with everything being shut up and locked?

*　*　*　*　*　*

It took a full two weeks to get someone to fix the air conditioning at Lynn's house. During that time Mark had called once. Not to see how she was doing but to see if the people had come yet to fix the system. Lynn tried to explain where she was and what had happened, but Mark made some excuses and then hung up. We went and checked her house regularly to make sure no one had broken in and to get more of Lynn's comfort things.

THE SKULL

Every time we arrived something changed. Lynn never seemed to notice. At first it was subtle – the mixer was on the counter instead of in the cupboard or there was a pile of papers sitting on the island. By the end of the two weeks, it had steadily escalated. Clothing tossed around the ground floor. The last time we went I opened the door first and there was an overwhelming smell of acetone. I told Lynn to go to the car and wait there. I called multiple people to find out who deals with toxic gases. Eventually the fire department showed up and with masks on went into the house. They found that there was a puncture in several of the tubes that fed the air conditioning into the house. Closer inspection found that all the fridges had their refrigerant leaking as well. They had opened the windows so the gas wasn't trapped anymore and were bringing in the right equipment to deal with it. We waited for a little while and then I took Lynn back home.

"That can't be a coincidence. Everything happening a day before the a/c guys were scheduled to fix it?" Jim was frowning deeply. I had insisted Lynn give me her house keys and go take a nap with a promise I'd go back over and wait for the fire department to finish up.

"I know but who'd want to hurt a sweet pregnant girl? Plus, she's not even staying there. She's been here with us for the last couple of weeks. It's probably just because everything got too hot in the house, and it couldn't take it anymore."

"We can go back over together. I want

to speak with the fire fighters. You can retrieve Lynn's stuff for her."

The fire fighters were just putting their equipment away on the truck when we arrived. Jim made a beeline for them as I headed for the open front door. There were a couple fire fighters standing on the porch still.

"Safe to go back in yet?"

"Yes Ma'am, we've cleared the gas out, it means you need to get some new fridges and freezers as well as a new a/c unit for the house. Looks like these were leaking all night. Lucky you weren't home when it happened."

"My sister's house. The a/c died a couple weeks ago and she's been staying with me in the heat. I made her go and lay down, she's about a month out from her due date and doesn't need to be stressed out. What happened to the fridges and freezers?"

"We probably shouldn't tell you this, but it looks like there were some drill holes in the lines. Not sure how they got there but the forensics team will look at them. The chief is listing it as arson. You won't be allowed to touch them yet. If there's anything you need we can walk you in to be sure that it's not part of the scene."

"Thanks – Lynn wanted her knitting and a few other small things to do when she's awake."

It took less than 5 minutes to get what Lynn wanted. We stood by the fire truck for another half hour while the police showed up. My favorite duo of Andrews and Dutch happened to catch the call.

"Still alive? Amazing! I've never met anyone that was so stubborn about not dying." Andrews started to laugh as he saw me standing there. The look on the fire fighters' faces was sheer confusion. I rolled my light sleeve up to show the skull.

"I'm not giving in that easy – you should know that by now Andrews."

"How long's it been? Five months?" Dutch chimed in.

"Six and a half. World's record. I plan on making it far longer too." We quickly filled Andrews and Dutch in on what had been happening with my sister and her husband. Along with the fact that she had been staying with me for the last couple weeks.

"Is it possible that someone saw Dawn going in and out of the house and decided that they had the time and opportunity to get another shot at her?" The look of concern and fear on Jim's face was heartwarming.

"Yeah, it's possible and since we know that she was involved we'll go over every possibility. I doubt that we will find anything though." Andrews sighed and shook his head. I gave Dutch the keys to Lynn's place and he went to make a copy so that they could access the house when needed.

"We'll let you know as soon as she can move back in." After giving Andrews all the information about when people were coming to fix the a/c system we went home. Lynn was sitting on the couch watching a show on tv. We sat down and explained everything to her, including my misgivings that it could have been my fault. She didn't take it

THE SKULL

well and ended up going to bed for the rest of the night. With so much going on at work Jim and I buckled down and tried to make some progress with the paperwork.

8 PLOTTING

Jim had heard from the air conditioning people. They had to replace the whole system. At this point we weren't surprised. Lynn and I went online and picked out the new fridges and freezers she wanted then placed the order. Shopping had made her feel much better about the situation. Andrews and Dutch came past to drop off the spare key for Lynn's house. They let us know they were done with the house but strongly suggested getting someone to clean the place professionally. I called around and made those arrangements without letting Lynn know I was paying for it.

I went a few days later and let the cleaners in. The fridges and freezers were due that evening. It looked like the police had dusted every inch of the house for fingerprints. While they cleaned I wandered around the house to make sure nothing had changed. There were no calls or contact from Mark during all of this. I'm not even sure he knew that Lynn was still staying with me. Jim had kindly been taking Lynn to counselling and had told me he'd already warned all his lawyers that he may need them to help her when the time came.

It was very kind of him, but Lynn was still holding out hope that she could reconcile with Mark. She'd confided in me that when she was able to go home she was going to arrange a night where she could confront him about his affair and make a stand about their marriage. I thought it was unwise to do it alone but that's what she wanted. After the cleaners moved up to the second floor I laid down on the couch on the ground floor and took a nap.

The next thing I knew I was being woken up to pay the cleaners. It cost a mint but was worth it. An hour later the delivery guys arrived and installed all the new fridges and freezers. By the end of the day Lynn would be able to come home and not have to worry about anything. I went to the grocery and bought a ton of food to fill everything again. I knew that it was a deep-seated feeling of guilt that made me pay for all the replacements. To be fair Jim had told me that the card Lynn had given him had been rejected when they'd run it for the air conditioning. He'd covered it himself and made me swear not to tell her. Sounded like Mark was not keeping up the payments and Lynn didn't know. I couldn't help but wonder if he was providing for his mistress and preparing for the time when he'd refuse to support Lynn and the baby.

* * * * *

It was nice to be back in my bed even if I did have to share it. Turns out that Jim snores. Not all the time but often enough to drive me up the wall. We were informed by Jim's lawyers that

Annie had finally signed the papers. Jim had gotten most of the assets in the marriage and had received the house. Annie was forcibly removed and caused a major scene for all the tabloids that were following her around from bar to bar.

Annie had received a nice sum of money for her part of the house and its contents. She was allowed to keep her personal items. Once she had vacated the house Jim moved back in, though he stated that he'd be coming over every weekend again.

It didn't matter to me – I had my house back to myself and it was wonderful! I was able to have a soak in the bath without worrying over how much water I was using. After a week the heat had eased off and I was in a much better mood. That's when the call came in and I had to rush over to Lynn's house. I called Jim to let him know that I wasn't going to make it in to work that day.

Lynn was sniffling. She hadn't stopped crying since I came over. She had confronted Mark about his affair. Things had gone downhill from there. Apparently, he had never wanted a child with anyone. He had proceeded to spew vile things to her about her looks and the baby. Lynn had refused to leave the house. Mark had stormed off with the threat that she had better not be there when he got back. She called me immediately.

Jim showed up with all his lawyers in tow. They went through the house with a fine-toothed comb. Since they had Lynn's permission, they started by going through his work files and personal files to see if he had any money or other assets hidden away. In the meantime, I sat with Lynn and let her cry all over me. I got up to grab some water and ran in to Jim in the kitchen on the first floor.

"How is she?"

"Not great. She seems to think that if she had just worked out more that she'd have stayed thin enough to keep Mark happy. Since I am pretty sure he was having this affair long before she started to get big with the baby, I know that there was nothing she could have done to change things."

"What do you mean you know how long he's been cheating," Jim made a gesture to the lawyers to join us.

"Well, I was talking with Lynn. The day that I got my skull on my arm is the day that I brought some food over for her and Mark. I thought it was them getting romantic in the guest room over there – turns out that is where she found the bra that wasn't hers. Pretty sure I accidentally walked in on him with his mistress. I didn't see anything that would tell me who she is, but I saw them."

"Can you give us the exact date? We can nail him for so much if we can show that this has been a long-term situation." One of the many lawyers was leaning forward eagerly.

"I don't recall the exact date off hand, but I remember that it was inventory day. The skull showed up back in February. Once I have access to my computer, I can pull the exact date up for you. I can even give you the approximate time. I stopped to get food for Lynn and I – fish and chips. Then I left it all here on the counter before walking home. Annie was staying with me at the time, and I wanted to delay my return home for as long as I could. I was a half a block up the street when the pain hit me."

"Why don't you and Jim go and get that info. There are security cameras all over this floor. They look like they hold over a year of footage. We can roll back and see who he was with, we may even be able to go far enough back to see when this started and how often it occurred." Lynn had a hollow empty look on her face. As soon as Jim and I were out the door I called our mother and had her come over to help Lynn feel better.

"This feels so surreal."

"I'd like to say bad things happen in threes but let's face it – you've had more than three bad things in the last few months. I'm sure your sister will be fine. These are the same lawyers that got me nearly everything in my divorce and I had gotten another woman pregnant." The seriousness in Jim's face and voice made me wince a little.

"True. I'm still worried about her though. I mean she's weeks away from having her baby, I still haven't thrown that damn party for her and now this on top of everything else? I don't know how much more I can take. Once the lawyers get what they need I want to set that trap we were talking about."

"Are you sure? We can't be certain that you will be safe when we try this." Jim had started having concerns about setting a trap when we were initially planning to set a trap before the heat had caused everything to get pushed off.

"It's time. Let's set the trap for this weekend. Less employees around easier to control everything. Please make the calls."

9 FINALE

Saturday came and I had made it known that I was going to be in the office all weekend catching up on things. Jim had put it out there that we needed to catch up so that we can start looking for an assistant for him starting Monday. Andy was given an extra day off since he'd been doing so much work covering Jim and I both. The new shop with specialty drinks had been a huge success and we were working on plans to expand the line to all our shops.

There were several security people that we'd brought in. They had required me to wear a wire the entire time I was in the office. Apparently if something did happen it could be used in court. As un-thrilled by this as I was everyone said that it was either wear the wire or don't go in to work. The excuse whenever someone asked was the tabloids had tried to sneak into the warehouse and Jim's house in an attempt to get more dirt. Word spread fast and we weren't disturbed after that. We had purposely left a hole in the security lay out with the hope that the killer would try to come through that way.

The wait was painful. I did manage to get caught up on all the paperwork. Once that was done, I sat and watched movies on my computer. Jim was in his own office down the hall. Annie was still part of the board for the company, but she'd signed paperwork saying that she wanted nothing to do with the day-to-day running of the business. Her office currently held some extra security guys including Dutch and Andrews. Apparently when Jim called Dutch to get things rolling again Andrews had been standing there and he wanted in.

I got up and went down the hall towards the washroom. No privacy at all. Everyone watched me walk there and back. This wasn't going to work. Surely the killer would see plain as day that I was protected and not bother taking a shot. I need to ditch these people to give the killer to me on a platter. The warehouse would be perfect. The day shift was heading off and we had stopped night shifts on weekends.

"I need to go down to the warehouse – I have to check the arabica order." I announced as I hit the button for the elevator. Dutch and a man named Simon followed me.

"You stay where we can see you at all times. How busy will it be down there?" Dutch was not happy with the change in venue.

"Should be deserted. I won't be long. I just noticed a difference in numbers on the paperwork from what was ordered to what was delivered. It should only be about ten minutes while I do a quick count."

"We'll do a walk through then you can do your work." The elevator doors opened. Dutch and Simon stepped out making their way around the exterior then up and down the rows. I wandered down the back aisle. It struck me that I rarely got to go down this way anymore. I took my time. The silence was so peaceful. For the first time in months, I felt calm and relaxed. I pulled out a piece of paper and pretended to count the large bags that were sitting on the shelving.

A flash of metal and a thunk into a bag next to me announced the arrival of the person that was after me. Coffee beans spilled everywhere across the floor as I stepped back trying to put some space between him and I. It was as if everything began to move in slow motion. My survival instincts kicked in. As the ax swung towards me again, I reached out grabbed the handle throwing my full weight to the opposite side of my attacker causing us both to fall in one direction and the ax to skid across the floor in the other.

He wasn't a very large man. This couldn't be the same person that had come at me originally. The man that had come after me had been much larger, heavier. I tumbled out from under him and came up to my feet. All I could do was bolt for the first hiding place I could think of – the shelves of coffee beans I had bounced off of. If I could just get to the area where we unload the trucks I could get the attention of my security detail. I managed to crawl through the shelves into the next aisle only to feel a hand grip my ankle tightly. With a quick yank I was back to where I had started only now my attacker had a solid hold on me. I aimed for his face and kicked as hard as I could in high heels. He dodged but lost his grip on me. Scrambling as fast as I could I managed to make the other side of the shelving and kicking off my shoes started to run down towards the doors hoping that Dutch was still checking the perimeter. No luck – just the man again. He seemed larger than before. How could that be? My mind must be playing tricks on me. I was far enough away; I spun and started heading back up the aisle. I could hear his shoes squeaking on the floor getting closer and louder as he closed the gap between us. Only one choice – back into the shelves. I only went halfway in. If I could slide between a few of these bags he may not see me. I don't think I'll ever like the smell of coffee again.

The shadow of his body passed in front of me a couple of times. Why did I have the urge to sneeze? It wasn't dusty! Working my way backwards I figured I should be able to get into the aisle behind me while he was still hunting the one in front. I felt with my feet for the floor and shifted as silently as I could out of the bags. I got grabbed from behind and tossed onto the floor. I saw stars and couldn't get a full breath. I rolled to my side and hit something solid. With a sinking in my gut I realized that I've hit my attacker in the side of the calves. Spinning quickly I turned on my hands and knees and kicked out causing him to hit the ground. A flash of blonde hair clued me in to who was under the hood.

"Annie?! Why??"

"Why?? My lover wasn't going to leave his wife. She would have gotten too much money. Especially after she got pregnant. I made plans to get rid of her. You just kept getting in my way. I couldn't be sure if you had recognized me that day when you dropped off the fish and chips for your sister. I tossed the food and note you left, just as an FYI. Mark was aware of my plans. I told him that I would have to get rid of you too. It was easy. All I had to do was hire a guy. Mark had the connections. How you managed to survive is beyond me. Seems the old adage is true – if you want something done right you have to do it yourself. I can see right there that you still have a skull on your arm. You know you'll never get out of here alive."

"Maybe. But I was always the one who

didn't believe that the tattoos dictate our fates. Something you should never have forgotten about me."

When I scrambled to get up Annie slid across the aisle and grabbed the ax again. She swung at me just as I ducked and stepped off the line of attack, narrowly avoiding getting hit in the head. We had forgotten about the coffee beans on the floor. She slipped and fell one way and I slid the other. The mic I had been wearing unclipped as I moved. My world narrowed to the fight with Annie. All I could do was keep moving. I felt blood trickling down my leg.

Then sirens became full volume as cars flew into the warehouse entrance. Everything became a blur. The police were everywhere. Annie was immobilized, then read her rights and cuffed while she cried and screamed about how I had attacked her and that she was the victim. It only stopped when she spotted Mark in the back of one of the cars. That's when she started screaming about how it was his fault and his idea. That he'd used her for his own nefarious needs.

I sat on the floor, tears sliding down my face. I couldn't stop shaking. It was over. Suddenly everything became filled with pain. My face had been scraped across the bags in the shelving, my knee was ripped open, I had bruises all over my body. My eyes searched the room looking for anyone that I knew. Jim was standing by the elevators. He was being kept there by a couple of officers. Dutch was on the ground his face beaten and tired. Simon was lying on the floor next to him, it looked like they had been in a fight as well. Of course, Mark. He'd been helping Annie. That's why I had seen my attacker on one side of the shelves then literally backed into him in the other.

All because I was doing something nice for my sister, I had become a target. I looked down at my arm. The skull was still there staring back at me mockingly. Once you received a tattoo it never disappeared. Even getting it removed made no difference, it would just come back. This would be a reminder for me. After all there couldn't be anyone else wanting to kill me, right?

EPILOGUE

The snow was settling around the trees in the backyard of my sisters' house. Little whale was giggling while playing with his feet as my sister watched smiling. The lights from the Christmas tree sparkled against the windows as the darkness deepened outside. It was just the three of us, we didn't talk about what had happened with Lynn's husband, Mark. Our mother and father were on a cruise that we'd bought as a gift that year for their anniversary. Nothing more romantic than a Caribbean cruise over Christmas. They hadn't known they'd be grandparents when they'd booked the travel dates. Once Mark and Annie were incarcerated a little whale had appeared on my mom's stomach right against the little kitten. Dad had sat back quietly while mom went crazy making party plans for her little kitten and little whale. We'd had it at my house. I spent weeks cleaning up the mess. Even now I think there is still some blue and silver glitter hiding in my couch cushions.

At first it was just a mild prickling on my arm. Exactly like when I'd first had my vine tattoos appear. Then the pain began to get worse. It was like someone was pressing a brand into my arm. I hit the floor as my legs collapsed underneath me. The skull disappeared. I'd never heard of a tattoo disappearing before. Once one appeared it stayed no matter what happened. Your tattoos told the story of your life. Suddenly there was an uptake in the pain again. Through the distortion that my tears were making I could see a new mark appear.

A target. Lynn had hold of my arm now. She was staring at me like she'd seen a ghost, "What does it mean?"

"I have no idea. I can only hope that no one else gets caught between me and whatever is coming for me." Slowly I shifted to look out the window again. The dampness on my cheeks eased though the ache in my arm remained. With a little luck the target would mean nothing more than I

THE SKULL

had survived.

But I wasn't born with a four-leaf clover. Luck was no friend of mine.

THE SKULL

ABOUT THE AUTHOR

No one reads this section anyways. I live. I write. That's all that matters. What do you really want? I love Mac and Cheese. Here's the recipe that Dawn uses in the story. Oh and no it's not healthy in the least and I don't care.

Ingredients:

2 Cups Macaroni

2 Tablespoons Butter (I use unsalted – cheese has lots in it)

2 Tablespoons Flour (All purpose or whatever you have is fine)

4 cups Cheese (I use 2 cups cheddar and 2 cups mozzarella)

2 cups milk

Pepper to taste

Pinch of Paprika (entirely optional)

Pot of water

Pot for the sauce

Casserole dish of some kind – I use a tall one.

Whisk and wooden spoons.

Oven to cook on and in

Process:

Grate up all your cheese first. That makes it easier later. Also 2 cups of each are relative – measure that shit with your heart. The reason for doing half mozzarella and half cheddar is so that the sauce has a nice melty cheese in it – this keeps the sauce smooth. At least that's what I've noticed. Put pot of water on to boil (every stove top is

different use common sense). In the
second pot melt butter on medium heat
(my stove this is a 5 or 6 setting for the
burner, every stove is different
exercise that common sense again).
Once the butter melts add the flour and
whisk till smooth but thick paste
forms. Let this cook for a minute – you
don't want it to brown or burn but you
don't want the flour flavor either. Add
half the milk to this mix and whisk till
nearly smooth. While this heats up add
your macaroni noodles to the water
and stir so they don't stick to the
bottom or each other. Set your timer
for 8 minutes and turn your water
down so it maintains a boil but doesn't
boil over. For me this means going
from max down to a 7 or 8 on the
burner. The milk should have started to
thicken. You don't want to boil it. Add
the rest of the milk and whisk till it

starts to thicken up again. I always forget to take the milk out so that it's room temp when adding it; this way stops it from splitting later.

Now occasionally stir your noodles – every 3ish minutes. You can tell the sauce is ready for the cheese if it coats the back of a spoon. I use a wooden spoon when I add my cheese, so I also use it to test the sauce, dip the spoon in and then hold it up and run a finger down the back. If the sauce parts and stays that way you're good to go. If not give it another minute or two. Add 1 cup of mozzarella and 1 cup of cheddar now. Stir this so it melts evenly. Once melted add another half cup of each and turn the heat off on the burner – leave pot on the burner so the cheese melts. This way it doesn't get too hot and spilt.

Your noodles should be done. Take them off the heat and turn that burner off (be careful: don't burn yourself!). Drain the noodles and place them in the casserole dish. Add the sauce. If all the cheese isn't fully melted that's ok. It's going in the oven briefly after this anyways. Now take the remaining cheese – or more if you want – and cover the top in cheese. Do the cheddar first as the flavor is stronger and mozzarella second (on top) since it's white it browns up and being a softer cheese strings way easier. Now pop that under your broiler for no more than 5 minutes depending on how deep you've got the cheese on there. Keep an eye on it as it will go from brown and beautiful to burned in seconds.

Take out of the oven and let stand for 5-10 minutes. I can never make it that

THE SKULL

long so just be careful not to burn yourself when you dig in.

There now you know something about me the Author. I like cheese.

Manufactured by Amazon.ca
Bolton, ON